A Scandal in Springtime

D1553174

A Scandal in

Springtime

A Pride and Prejudice Novel

LEENIE BROWN

LEENIE B BOOKS
HALIFAX

Contents

Dedication

To my niece Joy, who, like the heroine in this story, is taking her first steps into adulthood and who is just as sweet and sassy
May all the wonder, creativity, love, and enchantment that Kitty discovers in this story find its way into your future.
With all my love,
Leenie

Chapter 1

Kitty Bennet paused at the case containing the lace and brooches. There was a piece of lace intricately woven with leaves and flowers swirling along the edge and filling in the body which she would dearly like to purchase so that she could add it to her scarf. Just on the shelf above the lace was a brooch comprised of many tiny pearls which would be perfect for holding the scarf in place.

Perhaps next week when Uncle gave her the allowance her father had sent to him, she would have enough to purchase those two items so that she could wear them to church on Easter Sunday.

"Catherine."

Kitty jumped, her cheeks warming with embarrassment. "Forgive me, Uncle. I was distracted." Thankfully, even though her uncle had used her full name, he did not look put out. "That brooch is just so pretty," she added as she hurried to catch up to him.

"I am certain it is," he replied. "Although I am certain your aunt would know better, my dear."

"Do you think we can bring Aunt with us next time?"

The establishment through which they were walking was a new store that her uncle had said was nearly ready to open. And it appeared he was right, for the cases and shelves were filled with goods, the windows were being washed, and the floor looked as if it had already been polished.

Her uncle chuckled. "I am quite certain your aunt will demand it."

Kitty was not yet completely comfortable with her aunt and uncle – at least, not in the way her older sisters had always been. Jane and Elizabeth were always so at ease whenever the Gardiners visited Longbourn, but that was likely because they had spent so many visits with the Gardiners in town. However, now that her older sisters were married, that was about to change.

She and Mary were to take turns visiting their relations, for their mother hoped that in sending them to London, her remaining unattached daughters might happen upon some nice young gentle-men who would marry them and relieve Mrs. Ben-net of two more worries. There was no more signif-icant worry for a mother than to see her daughters well-cared-for. That is what Mama had always said.

Kitty put all thoughts of scarves and brooches, as well as handsome young gentlemen, away as she stood behind her uncle while he knocked at the door to the store's office before opening it when someone inside called *come in*.

"Mr. Gardiner, it is good to see you. With what can I help you?"

"Not a thing, Mr. Durward," her uncle replied. "My wife insisted that we deliver a basket of muffins to you as a gift of goodwill for the success of your store."

He looked at Kitty. "The basket," he whispered.

"I do apologize." Her cheeks burned once again with embarrassment, and she spared a quick glance for Mr. Durward. "I was distracted." How could she not be? The gentleman standing in front of the desk, the one who was not Mr. Durward, was far too attractive not to be distracting.

Her uncle chuckled. "This store seems to have that effect on you."

He took the basket from her and placed it on the desk. "There is one case containing brooches that my niece found of great interest. I think you will have a sale on your first day even if no one else enters the store."

"I am happy to hear it," Mr. Durward said with a friendly smile for Kitty. "Please be seated," he offered.

"I am afraid we are not able to stay today," Mr. Gardiner replied. "There are a few other errands which need our attention. However, Kitty and I wanted to see the basket delivered first." His brow furrowed. "I seem to have forgotten that you have not yet met my niece. This pretty young lady is Miss Catherine Bennet, and she is our houseguest for a few weeks this spring. Kitty, this is Mr. Durward and one of his partners, Mr. Waller."

Kitty dipped a curtsey. "It is lovely to meet you and to see your store. It is very well done up."

"Thank you," Mr. Durward replied, and Kitty found herself compelled once again to remove her eyes from Mr. Waller — handsome, tall Mr. Waller with his golden hair and piercing blue eyes.

"Have you settled into the apartment above?" Mr. Gardiner asked.

Mr. Waller lived here? Kitty's heart sank a trifle at the thought. She probably should not like him if he lived above a store. Mama might not approve.

"I have, and I have even employed a maid and a cook. It is a luxury I have not allowed myself until now. However, I think, even with the extra expense, I shall still be able to save the money I need to secure my future."

That seemed a funny thing for a gentleman to say, and Kitty wondered what it meant. However, she knew better than to ask. It was not right to be nosey, and while in town, Kitty intended to behave properly.

Here, she was not Lydia's sister. Indeed, she was no one's sister when she was alone with her aunt and uncle even if she still had to be Elizabeth's sister when she was attending one function or another with the Darcy's. However, it was not so bad to say that Mrs. Darcy was her sister for Mrs. Darcy was married. But Miss Kitty Bennet was not.

She was still thinking about how delightful it was to not be anyone's sister and have all the beaux to herself when her uncle said her full name – *Catherine* – once again.

"Forgive me," she muttered. She needed to work

on not looking like such a distracted fool – especially when in the presence of a very handsome gentleman like Mr. Waller. At least, she had not been caught admiring him.

"It was a pleasure to meet you, Mr. Durward, Mr. Waller," Kitty said in parting before preceding her uncle out of the office as he motioned for her to do.

"You are excessively distracted today," her uncle said as he wrapped her arm around his.

He was likely holding her hand on his arm to keep her from peering into any more of the cases. It was a far more enjoyable way to have one's attention focused than scolding or teasing ever was. She liked how her uncle patted her hand as if he enjoyed having her at his side.

"I get lost in my thoughts sometimes," she admitted.

"And are these happy thoughts?"

She nodded. "Sometimes they are about real life and other times they are about... well... a great number of things that are not real at all."

"Stories?"

She looked at her uncle. He seemed the sort of gentleman who would not make fun of a lady for being less intelligent than Elizabeth, but she was not entirely sure he would not tease her for dreaming up stories in her head. However, she nodded anyway. Lying was not proper, and in town, she was attempting to be proper.

"Would you like for me to stop at my warehouse and pick up a notebook for you in which to write these stories?"

"You would do that?" How shocking!

He nodded.

"You do not think it foolish of me to think up stories?"

He shook his head and held the door open for her. "Not at all. I quite enjoy reading."

So did Papa, but Kitty could not imagine him not saying writing stories was foolish. Stories did not seem to her to be scholarly enough to garner her father's approval. "They are very fanciful."

She waited for her uncle to change his mind about her thinking up stories, but he paid her no mind.

"We will be going to my warehouse," he told the driver before helping her into the carriage. "You do want the notebook, do you not?"

Kitty snapped her mouth closed and smiled while nodding. He was not going to change his mind. No wonder Elizabeth and Jane liked visiting Aunt and Uncle Gardiner so much!

"Uncle," she said as he took his seat, "I know it is not polite to inquire after things which are not my business, but I was wondering if it were possible for you to explain to me what Mr. Waller meant about saving to secure his future."

"Ah." Her uncle gave her a knowing look. "I am afraid that young man is well on his way to being married. He has only to earn enough money to please the young lady's father."

"Oh." That was disappointing. He was very handsome.

"I am sorry," Uncle Gardiner whispered.

"As am I," Kitty admitted. "His eyes are very blue."

Her uncle chuckled. "They are. However, I am certain you will meet with many handsome gentlemen while you are in town. Did you not dance with several when you attended that ball with Elizabeth?"

"Oh, I danced nearly every set and several of my partners were very handsome." She sighed. "However, none of them had eyes as blue as Mr. Waller's." She looked out the window at the passing buildings. Nor did any of them have hair the colour of spun gold.

"There is more to finding a good match than the colour of a gentleman's eyes," her uncle cautioned.

Kitty sighed. "I know. I must also consider his fortune."

"And his character," her uncle added with a raised brow. "No matter what your mother might tell you, a handsome character is far more important than a handsome fortune or face."

"Of course," she said quickly, her gaze dropping from looking at her uncle to her clasped hands.

"I am not reprimanding," Uncle Gardiner said softly. "At least, I am not reprimanding you. Your mother, however..." He chuckled. "She has raised five lovely daughters and prepared them quite well to oversee a household, but..." He paused. "Thinking deeply was never one of her strengths, and I fear, that in her exuberance to see you married to a husband who can keep you in fine dresses, she may have forgotten to instruct you about the qualities beyond face and fortune which qualify a gentleman as a good choice."

Kitty tipped her head and thought about that for a while. What had her mother taught her about how to choose a proper husband other than to seek one who was handsome and had a good income? Her eyebrows rose. Very little.

"I suppose he should be amiable," she said to her uncle. Mama did like agreeable gentlemen such as Mr. Bingley.

"That is a good quality," her uncle agreed. "Although amiability might be hidden at first."

Kitty nodded. "Like it was with Mr. Darcy."

Her uncle chuckled but did not disagree.

"Is there anything else you think a gentleman should be?" he asked.

She pulled her bottom lip between her teeth and sighed as she studied her gloved fingers. "I am not sure I know," she admitted with a shrug. "I wish for a handsome and amiable husband who has a good income."

The carriage began to slow. They were nearly to the warehouse.

"Those are excellent things for which to wish, but do not forget to find a gentleman who respects you and is kind."

"Oh, yes!" Why had she not thought of that? Of course, she did not want a husband who would make fun of her. Heaven knows she had endured enough of that in her life!

"And he should love you with his whole heart – to the point of death should he be separated from you."

Kitty blinked. She might have expected to hear such a statement from her aunt, but not from her uncle. He was a man. Men did not speak of such things. Did they?

"I see I have startled you," her uncle said. "I did not intend for my words to make you feel uneasy. I was just imagining what I would say to Priscilla if she were old enough to be seeking a husband."

He was thinking of her as his daughter? The idea wrapped around her, warm and comfortable, like a blanket made from the softest wool.

"At the risk of startling you more, that is how I feel about your aunt."

"It is?"

"Absolutely. I would be lost without her."

Oh, that was a very lovely thing! Kitty would most certainly like to marry a gentleman who felt that way about her.

"Then," Kitty said as the carriage door opened,

"I suppose I must find a husband who is very much like you."

Chapter 2

It did not take too terribly long for Uncle Gardiner to do the things which needed doing at his warehouse. There had been some papers that needed his signature and a question about some tables and where they were to be placed.

After those matters had been seen to, he had taken out a box of notebooks and allowed Kitty to choose one.

There had been several in that crate which she wished she would have been able to take home. However, this one, this plain notebook with its brown binding and floral cover, had seemed the best choice. The ornate notebooks with their attached pencils were beautiful, but they would garner far more attention and curiosity than this one, and they had also contained fewer pages, which would not do at all as she had so very many thoughts she wished to write down.

She ran her hand over the nondescript front of her notebook with satisfaction as she sat in the carriage while her uncle gave a few last instructions to a man about some delivery. Uncle Gardiner certainly was a very busy man — even on a day when he was not officially working.

It was very different from how her father did things. It was not as if her father never stirred from his study. He did. He rode around the estate a few times a week. However, a lot of his business was conducted from his study. He did not have men pushing carts and crates to and fro. Nor did he have urgent papers, which must be signed today, thrust at him when he walked into his book room.

It was a very different life here in town compared to Longbourn. Everything was busier. There were so many more people here than Kitty was used to seeing. The streets were crowded, and travel was not rapid at all. Not even in a carriage. Or, she thought as she saw a young boy carrying a parcel race past, perhaps it was because they were in a carriage that travel was so slow. Be that as it may, she was positive she did not wish to be walking from place to place here, for there were so many streets she was sure to get lost.

"If you had a pencil, you could begin a story now," her uncle said as they started moving down the street. "I am anxious to read one."

Kitty smiled and blushed. "I am not certain they will be good enough to justify your anticipation." She had never before put her imagining down on paper. She was not even certain she knew how to do it, but she was determined to try.

"What shall the first one be about?" Her uncle looked out the window. "How about that man there? The one walking with the stuttering gait. He seems an interesting character."

Kitty pressed her nose against the glass to look back at the man. "Oh, he is interesting!" she cried. "Look at his coat. It looks as if it could have been a very nice coat at one time."

"But was it his when it was so fine, or did it belong to another?" Mr. Gardiner's eye sparkled with amusement. It was as if he was enjoying this game as much as she was.

"I think it must be a tragic story if it was his." She pursed her lips and furrowed her brow as she thought.

"Or," her uncle said, "it could be a disguise."

Kitty's eyes grew wide, and she could not help smiling from the excitement such a thought sent skittering across her skin. But the man's coat was not a disguise, as delicious as that idea was.

"A curse!" she cried. "He has been cursed by a princess and is doomed to wander the world in rags and with a hole in his boot – that is why he walks as he does – until he has paid his dues for some ill behaviour. Oh! I do wish I had a pencil!"

Mr. Gardiner chuckled. "And I must say my anticipation to read your story is growing by the minute. I should very much like to know what this gentleman did to receive his curse."

"That is a very good question." She had not thought that far into the story.

"His penance must be appropriate to his sin," her uncle added, his own brow furrowed as if he were actually contemplating something as fanciful as a story, which was both an odd and a delightful thing to Kitty.

"If he has stolen something or treated someone unjustly," Kitty said, "then he might have to restore four times the value of the stolen item or must endure life as the servant of an ogre until he can serve such a master with equanimity."

Her uncle nodded his head. "Those are excellent thoughts, but, unfortunately, we will have to continue our story later for I see Mrs. Verity's house from here. Do you have the items your aunt wished us to give to Mrs. Verity?"

Kitty placed her notebook on the bench next to her, tucked her story away in her mind, and picked up the parcel with the yellow ribbon.

~*~*~

"These are exceptional, as always," Mrs. Verity said after opening the package Kitty had given her. "But then, I have come to expect nothing less than exceptional from your aunt."

"She is very good at sewing," Kitty agreed. "I hope one day I can sew as neatly as she does."

"I hear you do very well now," her uncle said. "Your aunt has told me so," he added in response to her startled look. "Your mother has taught you well."

"Oh, it was not Mama who taught me," Kitty replied. "It was Jane."

"Indeed?"

Kitty nodded. "Mama was busy with Lydia."

"My sister has five daughters," Mr. Gardiner explained to Mrs. Verity.

"That is a lot of young ladies to teach." She winked at Kitty. "I should know. We have more than five here, but I am fortunate to have several helpers." She rose. "Would you like to meet my young men and ladies?"

"Oh, very much!"

"These," she said, tapping the papers Mr. Gardiner had given her, "I will look at later over a cup of tea. There are no surprises here, are there?"

"No, those are the particulars about the two apprenticeships that my wife told you about last time she was here. She would have brought them here herself, but..." He followed behind Mrs. Verity. "I had several things that needed doing today, and it is not often I get to spend the day with any of my nieces. It has been most pleasurable. However, I wonder if I might put upon both of you to accommodate me with something."

"Most certainly," Kitty said without hesitation. How could she not oblige him after he had been so generous in giving her a notebook and so understanding about her love of creating stories? He had endeared himself to her in a way that no one else had ever done by showing such interest in things that she liked.

"I have one more delivery to make to a gentleman only a few streets from here, and I was thinking that instead of hurrying Kitty through a tour, it might be better if she were to spend an hour and a half or thereabouts with you while I see to my delivery and return. She is very good with her cousins. I am certain your young ones would get on capitally with her."

Kitty sucked in a breath and waited to be granted permission to stay for so long. Elizabeth had told her about this place, and she was eager to see it.

"We are always happy to have willing volunteers," Mrs. Verity said. "I rarely send away anyone who wishes to help." She nodded to a handsome gentleman who had just entered the corridor.

"Mr. Edwards," Mr. Gardiner greeted. "The new tables have arrived."

"Excellent!" Mr. Edwards replied. "We shall soon be able to feed everyone in one sitting instead of two."

"It will be more efficient," Mr. Gardiner agreed.

Kitty looked from her uncle to the handsome

gentleman speaking to him and back. What on earth were they talking about? Why was this gentleman, who was dressed as well as Mr. Darcy ever dressed, talking to her uncle about tables?

"Forgive me, Kitty. I see I have confused you."

Well, he did not need to point out her confusion in front of a stranger – especially a very attractive one who looked rather wealthy!

"You remember my telling you about the charity that has been started at my warehouse?"

Oh! She did remember that. "The one where you feed people?"

"The very one. Mr. Edwards was the gentleman who pressed me into starting it. He has a fondness for doing charitable work." Her uncle smirked. "Due entirely to a young lady who he will soon call his wife."

Kitty's eyes grew wide. "Indeed?" Were all the handsome gentlemen in London who her uncle knew married or nearly so? It was no wonder it took Jane so long to find a husband.

"They became betrothed in my office at the warehouse," her uncle whispered loudly.

"Oh! That was you?" she asked Mr. Edwards. She had heard the story from her aunt.

Mr. Edwards smiled broadly. "It was."

He looked as proud and happy as any person could ever look. It was just how Kitty hoped a gentleman might one day look when saying she was his betrothed. She sighed wistfully. "It is a beautiful story."

"Mr. Edwards," Mr. Gardiner said, "this is my niece, Miss Catherine Bennet. Kitty, this is Mr. Edwards, although I suppose you have already figured that out." He chuckled. "I am dreadful at introducing people before entering into a conversation."

"It is a pleasure to meet you, Miss Bennet," Mr. Edwards said with a shallow bow. "If you will pardon my saying so, you look slightly familiar."

"That is because she is Mrs. Darcy's sister," Mrs. Verity said.

"Yes, yes, that is it! You do bear a resemblance to Mrs. Darcy."

"You know her?"

"I met her right here. In this very spot."

"Your boys are waiting," Mrs. Verity said.

"Excellent." Mr. Edwards clapped his hands together and then rubbed them back and forth. "If you are giving a tour, Mrs. Verity, you will wish to skip that room for today, I am to undress and allow them to help me back into my clothes without any instruction."

Kitty's mouth popped open at his shocking words.

"I do apologize, Miss Bennet. I know that was not very proper of me to say in front of a young lady such as yourself. However, I am not very proper."

Mrs. Verity laughed. "That you are not," she said to his retreating form. "Until Miss Barrett came along, I understand he was quite a rake."

"He was a rake?" Kitty had never seen a rake before. She had heard of them, but there were none in Meryton.

"Very much so," her uncle said with a note of caution in his tone. "Town is much different than the country."

"Apparently so," Kitty agreed. "Lydia will be jealous that I have seen a rake and she has not." She pressed her lips together. That was not the thing to say. "I did not mean that we wished to see one or... or... fall prey to one," she muttered.

"All is well," her uncle said. "Just be aware that

a rake looks very much like any other gentleman. However, he behaves far less properly."

"I will keep her safe," Mrs. Verity put an arm around Kitty's shoulders and directed her away from the door and down the hallway. "Not that Mr. Edwards has a thought in his head about young ladies these days save for the one to whom he is betrothed. However, he is still improper at times – shockingly so." She chuckled. "He is also very good with two of my older boys and is training them to be butlers and valets."

She removed her arm from Kitty's shoulder and opened a door. "This is the dining room. The children take turns being both the servers and the served in this room. It is important for them to see both sides of the table."

"It is beautifully furnished," Kitty said, strolling into the room to look at the paintings on the wall. "I should very much like to have a dining room such as this in my home."

"Thank you, Miss Bennet." Mrs. Verity was smiling warmly and looking at the dining table with pride in her eyes. "This was the table my husband purchased during our first year of marriage."

Kitty ran a finger along the curved mahogany edge. "He had very good taste."

"He did."

Kitty's companion now wore a faraway expression as Kitty took her time looking at the various dishes and furnishings of the room while supposing that Mrs. Verity was thinking of her husband. She must have loved him very much to look as she did now with that small smile on her lips and the softness in her eyes.

"The room across the hall is used as a classroom," Mrs. Verity said when they exited the dining room. "Mr. Darcy often reads to the children in that room when he visits."

That was surprising. "Is he a good reader?"

"Oh, very. The children hang on his every word."

To Kitty, it was hard to imagine Mr. Darcy reading to children, let alone, in such a fashion as to entertain them, but then, he was so much different now than he had been when she first met him.

"Do you read well, Miss Bennet?" Mrs. Verity looked at the watch which hung on her chatelaine.

Kitty nodded. "I often read to the tenants' children when I accompany Mama on her visits."

"Well, then, you are just in time. I will introduce you."

Chapter 3

"You read very well."

"Thank you," Kitty said with a smile for the pretty young lady who had joined her and Mrs. Verity in the younger children's room while Kitty was reading.

"If Miss Linton is here," said Mrs. Verity, "then it must be time for tea. Shall we retire to my office or the drawing room?" She gave a nod to the children's teacher, who immediately came to take Kitty's book and to send the children to the tables.

"The drawing room," Miss Linton said.

"Excellent choice," Mrs. Verity agreed. "We shall finish our tour after we have had some tea," she assured Kitty before leading them out the door and down the hall toward the front of the house. "The drawing room is set aside for our guests."

She thanked the butler, who she called Smith,

for opening the drawing-room door and then asked him to see that tea was brought in directly.

Kitty followed behind Miss Linton and took a seat next to her by the window.

"Miss Linton, now that there are no children gathered around our feet, allow me to introduce you to Miss Bennet. Her uncle is Mr. Gardiner, and he has allowed me the privilege of keeping her for a short time while he conducts some business."

Mrs. Verity had a very pleasant manner, for she made Kitty feel entirely at ease with just a few words.

"And Miss Bennet, this is Miss Linton, who volunteers here at least twice each week at present, but she will soon marry, and then that will change."

"You are betrothed?" It seemed to Kitty as if everyone she was going to meet today was happily matched. Perhaps she had arrived in London too late in the season.

"I am," Miss Linton answered.

"Mr. Crawford, Miss Linton's betrothed is a particular friend of Mr. Edwards, whom you met earlier."

"Oh." It was all Kitty could think to say as she

wondered if this Mr. Crawford was also a rake like his friend.

Miss Linton did not appear to be the sort of lady who would court a rogue. She sat just as she should, and she had not once spoken out of turn or put herself forward.

"Since December, I have been very successful in seeing three ladies, who have come to volunteer here, happily betrothed," Mrs. Verity said with a laugh. "Not that any of it was my doing, of course. I just happened to be fortunate enough to meet them. I am no matchmaker. However, I might begin to think of myself as good luck, especially if we can see Miss Bennet well-matched."

"Oh, that would be lovely," Kitty agreed. "I should like to find a husband. It is why my mother has sent me to town, and why Mr. Darcy is taking me to soirees."

"Miss Bennet is Mrs. Darcy's sister," Mrs. Verity said to Miss Linton. "And, she has three other sisters, is that not correct?"

"Indeed, it is," Kitty said. "Jane is the oldest and has married Mr. Bingley." She paused for a moment as Mrs. Verity instructed the maid in how to set up the tea.

The young girl was likely just learning how to perform the service as an older, more experienced looking maid stood behind her.

Once the tea was successfully arranged, Kitty continued while Mrs. Verity poured.

"Mr. Bingley is Mr. Darcy's particular friend, and I must say, he is likely one of the most amiable gentlemen in all of England. After Jane, is Elizabeth. She is now Mrs. Darcy. And then, there is Mary, me, and Lydia. Mary shall have her turn in town at Christmas. She was ill, and so I was sent in her place."

"I hope it was nothing serious," Miss Linton said.

Kitty shook her head. "Just a mild fever and sore throat. Mary is very good about taking all her medicine, so I am certain she will be well before Mama's first letter arrives."

"That is good, then," Miss Linton took a sip of her tea. "Are you all very close in age? I only have a brother and have always thought it would be lovely to have a sister."

"It is not always lovely," Kitty replied, causing Mrs. Verity to chuckle. "In fact," Kitty continued, "I will likely sound dreadful for admitting it, but it has been rather pleasant to be at Aunt and Uncle Gardiner's without a single sister. I love them dearly, but well, yes, we are all close in age, and it is sometimes trying to be noticed. Or, at least, it is for me. And Mary."

"But not your other sisters?" Miss Linton asked.

"Jane is beautiful. Lizzy possesses a quick wit and is second in beauty to Jane. And Lydia?" Kitty smiled. "Lydia will not be overlooked. It is just not possible."

"Miss Lydia is lively, is she?" Mrs. Verity asked.

"Oh, very!" Kitty's youngest sister was nearly always in a state of animation about something.

She turned to Miss Linton. "I have no brothers," Kitty said. "What is it like to have one?"

"I suppose it depends on the brother," Miss Linton said. "Mine is my guardian."

Kitty sucked in a quick breath. How sad!

"He has my aunt to help him. Not that he would need much help. Trefor is exacting and excessively proper, which suits me quite well most times. However, he can occasionally be a trifle too unwavering. That is where Aunt Gwladys' help becomes invaluable."

"Will you miss them greatly when you marry?"

Kitty knew she would miss her mother and sisters. Longbourn had felt odd without either Jane or Elizabeth there. How lonely Mama and Papa would be once they were all married!

Miss Linton drew and released a breath as if taking off a heavy mantle. "I will, and I would feel much better about leaving them both if Trefor were to marry. But he says he is not ready for that."

"That is what they all say until they have met just the right lady," Mrs. Verity inserted.

"He has not met the right lady then," Miss Linton said with a laugh. "Not that my aunt has not done her best to suggest which lady might be right for him." She turned back to Kitty after placing her cup on the table. "Trefor is also a good friend of Mr. Crawford and Mr. Edwards."

"How..." Kitty clamped her lips shut. She should not ask what she wished to know. She was attempting to be proper while in town and being inquisitive about things which were not necessary for her to know was not proper. Mary had told her that many times.

"That is a good question," Miss Linton replied with a smile. "I have always wondered why they became friends, but I suppose it goes back to school days before either Mr. Crawford or Mr. Edwards took up their charming ways."

The need to ask about Mr. Crawford was nearly overwhelming.

"You may ask what you will," Miss Linton said. "I can see that you are curious about something." She leaned a bit closer to Kitty. "I will admit to being improperly inquisitive on occasion – especially when there is something of interest about which I wish to learn. Trefor is forever scolding me about asking him things he thinks are not appropriate. So, please ask me whatever it is you wish to know."

"Are you certain?" Kitty asked. "I am attempting to behave as well as I can, but I must confess it is not easy to quell one's curiosity."

"I am positive." Miss Linton looked expectantly at her, making Kitty feel somewhat better about asking what she was about to ask.

"My uncle said that Mr. Edwards was a rake..." Kitty ran a finger around the rim of her cup. "So, I was thinking, if he is a rake and you have said both he and Mr. Crawford are charming, does that mean Mr. Crawford is — was — also one?"

Miss Linton nodded. "He was, but his unscrupulous ways led him to heartbreak which, in turn, led him to wish to change his ways and that, led him to ask me to help him." She shrugged, and a smug grin settled on her lips. "I did a very good job of teaching him how to be a proper gentleman, and my friend was nearly as successful with Mr. Edwards, although I do not suppose Mr. Edwards will ever be entirely proper."

This was all very fascinating and novel information.

"I had thought that rakes were not capable of changing." Was that not what Mama had declared over and over after Mr. Wickham had been sent away?

Her daughters were to beware of such fellows for they were only ever capable of leading a lady to misery.

Of course, Mama had not been able to answer Mary's question about how to know if a gentleman was merely amiable or was a charmer, so between not knowing that and now knowing what she knew about Mr. Crawford and Mr. Edwards, it seemed, there was still much Kitty needed to learn about such gentlemen.

"I would like to think that no one is incapable of

change," Mrs. Verity said. "However, it does seem an impossibility for some. I think, and this is only my supposition, of course, but to me, it seems that both Mr. Crawford and Mr. Edwards were not without a good heart buried under their deviant ways. For, if they were corrupted through and through, I doubt they could have retained Mr. Linton's friendship."

"I am sure you are correct," Miss Linton agreed. "As a rule, my brother is not very tolerant of improper behavior."

"From what I understand," Mrs. Verity continued, "change was not without some degree of pain for either of them." She placed her empty cup on the table. "Which, in my opinion, is as it should be. One must suffer the consequences of one's poor decisions to some extent, depending upon how much the good Lord requires."

She pushed up from her chair. "Shall we complete our tour now, Miss Bennet? And then, when we are finished, we will join Miss Linton again while we await your uncle."

For the next twenty minutes, Kitty followed Mrs. Verity up stairs and down corridors, looking into various rooms and hearing the purpose of each.

When the upper levels had been seen in nearly their entirety, save for the one room where two boys named Arthur and Stephen were receiving instruction from Mr. Edwards, Kitty and Mrs. Verity descended into the basement to view the kitchen.

The aroma of roasting meat mixed with that of the fresh bread on the workbench as Kitty stood listening to Mrs. Verity explain how the girls would begin their lessons in the scullery before moving up to assist the cook. Despite the biscuit Kitty had eaten with her tea, her stomach could not ignore the tantalizing smells around her and protested her lack of indulgence in those tasty morsels by rumbling.

Mrs. Verity smiled. "I think a few treats might be nice to have while we sew." She took a tin from the cupboard and handed it to Kitty. "I need to speak to the cook for a moment. Do you remember the way to the drawing room? If not, you may wait here."

"No, I remember."

"Then, will you think me very rude to send you up to Miss Linton without me?"

"Not at all," Kitty assured her. "I would be delighted to be of service."

Mrs. Verity patted Kitty's forearm, gave her a warm smile, and then, turned back to her cook, who was waiting with a book of receipts in hand, while Kitty made her way out of the kitchen, past the servant's hall and the butler's rooms to the stairs that led up to the ground floor.

She was just about to enter the drawing room when the door opened, and a gentleman stepped out. Perhaps if she had not been so distracted by how tall and broad he was or by his light brown hair that fell in waves, she might have been able to move out of his way before he crashed into her. But, sadly, she had been distracted by the hand-some stranger, and so it was that she ended up stumbling and nearly falling. Thankfully, she caught his arm and kept her feet. Unfortunately, the tin of biscuits was lost in the action. Biscuits tumbled across the floor as the tin clattered and skipped before coming to a stop.

"My apologies," his voice was deep and wonderfully smooth. Kitty imagined it was what caramel might sound like if it had a voice – rich and sweet.

He bent and retrieved the biscuit tin which lay at his feet. "I shall gather the large pieces while you retrieve a broom, and I will be sure to tell Mrs. Verity that you were not at fault. You should not be punished for my clumsiness."

Kitty's mouth dropped open. He expected her to get a broom? Did he think she was a maid?

"I am sure I do not know where there is a broom." She lifted her chin and affected her most Lydia-like look of disdain. How dare he think she was a servant! Could he not see that she was dressed in a proper lady's blue day dress?

"You do not know where there is a broom?" He looked at her as if she was the most absurd person he had ever met. "How do you not know?"

"I do not know," she said as she folded her arms, "because I, like you, am a guest here."

His hand froze over the biscuit he was about to pick up. "You are a guest?" It sounded as if he were choking on the words which made Kitty smile as she answered, "yes."

"Ah, Miss Bennet!" Mr. Edwards cried as he

came down the stairs followed by two young boys. "How do I look?"

"Fully clothed," she answered before she could stop the words from popping out of her mouth. Her cheeks burned as Mr. Edwards' laughed. "And not any different than you did when you arrived," she added. "I believe your students have done an excellent job." Her insides fluttered and flopped with embarrassment. She had been doing so well at being proper until now.

"And these are the fine young fellows who have recreated such perfection," Mr. Edwards said, motioning to the boys behind him. "This is Stephen on the right, and this is Arthur on the left. Lads, this is Mr. Gardiner's niece, Miss Bennet."

"It is a pleasure to meet you, Miss Bennet," Arthur said.

Stephen nodded his head and muttered his agreement.

"I think he is a bit smitten with you," Mr. Edwards, who had crossed the corridor to where Kitty was, whispered. "Not without reason," he added.

Kitty did not know exactly what to say to such a thing but managed to stammer a thank you.

"Linton," Mr. Edwards said to the gentleman picking up biscuits. "Here to collect your sister?"

"*You* are Miss Linton's brother?" Kitty asked in surprise.

The gentleman rose from his crouched position as he nodded.

"You are not at all like her."

"I think I am," he said.

"She would not ask me to get a broom."

Mr. Edwards chuckled.

"You were carrying a tin, and you're wearing blue."

Kitty's mouth popped open, but she quickly closed it while she scowled at him. "And you are wearing black, does that make you a coachman?"

"I have no horses with me," Trefor argued.

"And I have no broom."

"I do, Miss Bennet," Stephen said.

Kitty smiled at him. "Thank you. That is very thoughtful." She took the broom from the lad and handed it to Mr. Linton. "Your broom," she said, and then with a flip of her head, she stepped past him and into the drawing room.

Chapter 4

Trefor Linton stood looking at the drawing-room door which had closed soundly behind the pretty young woman he had assumed was a maid.

"Do you know how to use that?" Charles Edwards pointed to the broom Trefor held.

"Yes," Trefor snapped. "I am not stupid."

"Shall I verify that with Miss Bennet?"

"I'll thank you to leave off with your teasing." Trefor handed the tin he held to Charles. "You may eat them if you do not mind a bit of dust."

"I am not going to eat biscuits which have been on the floor."

"I can sweep for you, mister," Stephen said.

Trefor shook his head. "Thank you, but I shall see to it."

As much as he wished to let the lad clean up the mess he had made, Trefor was not the sort of gentleman to shirk any responsibility – most especially a task that he doubted Miss Bennet would believe he would or could do. She likely *expected* him to pawn the job off on a servant.

"That was not a very good first impression," he muttered.

"No, sir," Stephen, who stood by holding a dust-pan, answered. "She was rather put out with you."

Trefor held his mouth firmly closed to keep from uttering some retort, which would likely be something rather rude, seeing as he was also feeling *rather put out.*

"She was wearing blue." He cast a look at his friend. He was uncertain if he were trying more to convince himself or his friend that his assumption had not been as wrong as it was. The fact did nothing to assuage his feelings of guilt for having insulted a lady. He did not do that. He always spoke to ladies properly.

"Many ladies do wear that colour, and if you had paused to notice, it was made of a very fine muslin." Charles leaned against the wall next to the drawing-room door. "And I must say she wore it well."

Trefor glared at his friend.

"I was only commenting on what was obviously apparent to everyone save you."

"She is rather shorter than taller."

"Your logic is still flawed."

Trefor motioned for Stephen to lend his aid with the dustpan.

"I do not know everyone who is here. She seemed the right size for some of the young ladies who live here."

"She's about as tall as Susan," Arthur inserted. "Susan is going to have an employer soon," he added to Charles. "Your Miss Barrett said so last week."

Charles grinned broadly. "Then, I would imagine it is a good home to which Susan is going."

"She's awful excited," Arthur said. "She'll have her own money soon and a place to live and all that."

"It is a good thing," Charles assured him.

"We'll miss her, of course," Arthur added.

Charles scruffed the lad's hair and merely smiled. He was at ease no matter where he was. Trefor supposed that was likely due to his friend's lack of care for rules and boundaries. Edwards was like a river that flowed over flat river beds as easily as it slipped over the edge of a waterfall and through the boulders in a rapid. Trefor was more like basin of water, staying within its designated confines and seeing to whatever duty for which it was deemed necessary. And creating a fine mess when tipped over, he thought as he scowled at the broom in his hand. He positively felt tipped over.

"Susan proves my logic was not entirely faulty." Trefor spared a glance at his friend, who merely smiled and shook his head.

"Not much left for the mice," Trefor said with satisfaction after giving the floor a thorough look-ing over.

"You did a fine job, sir," Stephen assured him. "I didn't know a gentleman in fancy dress could do such a good job and almost not soil his clothing."

Trefor's brows furrowed.

Stephen pointed to Trefor's breeches.

With a sigh, Trefor smacked at the dust on his knees. He was certain that he had never before got-ten dust on the knees of his breeches when calling on someone. It was just another way in which he felt completely turned on his head.

"You look presentable enough to be properly

introduced to Miss Bennet now," Charles said with a laugh.

"I already know who she is," Trefor protested. "Gardiner's niece. I shall await my sister in the carriage as was planned."

"Mr. Linton," Mrs. Verity greeted. "Are you here so soon to steal away your sister?"

"I am. Our aunt reminded me of an engagement we are to keep tonight."

"And what have we here, boys?" she asked Stephen and Arthur.

"Miss Bennet dropped her tin of biscuits," Arthur said. "And we were helping clean them up."

Mrs. Verity looked to the older gentlemen to confirm the boy's words.

"It was I who caused the destruction of the biscuits," Trefor admitted. "I was not paying close enough attention when I exited the drawing room."

He had been thinking of that blasted soiree which his aunt insisted he attend and which he had no desire to attend. He had been, in fact, in a foul mood, which was why he had not wished to stay in the drawing room with his sister and wait for Mrs. Verity. He had only wished to deliver his message to his sister and be gone.

He had not even particularly wished to see Charles, though he had known his friend was upstairs. Charles would be altogether too happy to be going to this particular soiree, for according to Aunt Gwladys, both of his good friends, Charles and Henry, would be there since Constance and her friend, Charles's betrothed, would also be there.

Trefor was in no hurry to marry, but he had to admit that it was becoming less and less pleasant to be the only single gentleman of his set of friends. And his conniving aunt knew it! He was certain of that fact. It was why she was so eager to have him escort her to this poetry reading tonight.

Poetry! He barely refrained from rolling his eyes at the thought. It was not as if he had anything against poetry. He actually enjoyed reading it. However, having to sit in a room as an unattached gentleman of good fortune and standing while simultaneously listening to poetry and being eyed by hopeful matrons and their charges was the surest way to drive any love of poetry from a gentleman.

"Then you have met my guest?" Mrs. Verity asked.

"Not formally," Trefor admitted.

"I was just about to make the introduction," Charles said, opening the door to the drawing room.

Trefor's eyes narrowed. He wished to retort that he was not returning to the drawing room, but that would be impolite to do in front of Mrs. Verity. He had already offended one lady today. He did not need to make it two.

"I understand we had a little mishap with the biscuits," Mrs. Verity said as she entered the room ahead of Charles and Trefor.

Miss Bennet blushed prettily. "I must apologize for that."

"No, no, it was my fault," Trefor interjected.

"It was most certainly mostly your fault," Miss Bennet replied, her chin lifting, "but it was not entirely your fault. There is no need to be gallant on my behalf, sir. I sometimes get lost in my thoughts," she added to Mrs. Verity. "I will own that it is a dreadful habit."

Her eyes darted quickly toward him and Charles.

"Accidents do occur now and then," Mrs. Verity said. "However, I understand that due to the unfortunate events in the corridor, a formal introduction was never made. Miss Bennet, this is Miss Linton's brother, Mr. Trefor Linton, and Mr. Linton, this is Miss Catherine Bennet. If you are to be here often, Miss Bennet – which I assume you will be since your aunt and your sister both are here regularly — you will likely meet on occasion, and it is much more pleasant when each knows the other."

From the expression Miss Bennet wore, Trefor could tell that pleasant was not the word she would use to describe their knowing one another.

"And if you are to call on me," Constance said, "it is best that you know who my brother is."

"Call on you?"

"Yes, brother dear, I was just inviting Miss Bennet to call on me. I think we shall be good friends. I honestly cannot wait to introduce her to Aunt Gwladys and Evelyn."

"Her uncle is a tradesman. Do you think he will have the opportunity to deliver her to our house?" His brow furrowed when he saw Miss Bennet fold her arms as she had in the hallway. "I am not opposed to having Miss Bennet call. I was merely concerned that it would take him away from his work."

"I make calls with my sister," Miss Bennet replied primly.

"Very good then. As long as it will not inconvenience your uncle." For some reason, Trefor felt well out of his depth in this conversation, which was not a normal thing for him. "I must apologize once again for my assumption earlier." He felt his ears growing hot.

"I shall not wear blue when I call on your sister to save you any confusion."

Her lips pressed together, and she ducked her head as if she was embarrassed about what she had said.

"I shall not make the same mistake twice," he assured her. "Wear whichever colour you like. Blue is nice." Charles had not been wrong in his assessment of Miss Bennet wearing her dark blue dress well. The colour looked lovely against her creamy complexion, and the fit was exceptionally good for it flattered her curves in a most distracting fashion.

She smiled at him. "It is a favourite colour."

"What is?" He could not for the life of him

remember what colour had been mentioned now that she was no longer scowling at him.

"Blue," she said. "You just said blue was a nice colour." She cast a worried glance at Constance.

"Oh, yes, right," he stammered. "I am not usually so scattered."

"Neither are the biscuits," Charles whispered before chuckling.

Trefor rose. "I shall wait for you in the carriage, Connie." He needed to get out of this house before he made an even greater fool of himself. "We have that poetry reading tonight."

"Oh, are you going to that, too?" Miss Bennet asked Constance eagerly. "It will be so nice to know someone there."

"You are going to it?" Trefor asked.

Miss Bennet's head bobbed up and down. "With my sister."

His brows furrowed. How had nieces of the Gardiners received invitations to such a soiree? His eyes grew wide as he realized Miss Bennet was once again scowling at him.

"Mr. Gardiner is my uncle not my father."

"Yes, yes, I know," Trefor defended.

"Do you think I am a tradesman's daughter?"

She was rather direct in the questions she asked! Was she not aware that a young lady was supposed to demur politely by turning the conversation? That was what they were supposed to do, was it not?

Trefor swallowed and smiled sheepishly. "At the risk of offending you yet again, yes."

Her hazel eyes rolled upward as she huffed in exasperation.

"Your father is a gentleman?" he asked quickly.

Mrs. Verity chuckled. "He is, indeed, as is her sister's husband."

"You know him?"

"Not her father," Mrs. Verity clarified, "but yes, I know Mr. Darcy."

Trefor blinked. "Mr. Darcy?"

"Do you know him?" Miss Bennet asked.

Trefor shook his head. "I have never met him, but I know who he is."

"And does *he* meet with your approval?"

Again, she pressed her lips together as if she were frustrated, and his conscience pricked him because he knew he was the cause of her consternation. He blew out a breath. "Yes. But then, so does Mr. Gardiner." He bowed to her. "Until this evening."

And with that, he made as quick an escape as one could make when one was attempting to walk sedately out of the room.

Chapter 5

"I will be surprised if Miss Bennet does call on me." Constance glanced at her brother before taking another bit of her meal.

"Why is that, dear?" Aunt Gwladys asked. "She sounds like a delightful young lady."

Trefor raised an eyebrow at his sister. He suspected he knew exactly where she was going with this conversation. He was about to be reprimanded yet again for his poor behaviour at Mrs. Verity's. He deserved it, but he did not appreciate it.

"Trefor was rather condescending," Constance replied.

"Our Trefor was condescending? To a lady?"

He could not fault his aunt's look and tone of utter incredulity. He was ordinarily polite to a fault when in the presence of a young lady. His father had taught him to be a gentleman, and he had always striven to be the man his father wished him to be.

"More than once," his sister said.

"I was in a foul mood." It was a pathetic excuse, but it was also the truth.

"And what accounts for your foul mood?" His aunt placed her cutlery on her plate and, taking up her glass of wine, settled back in her chair with an expectant look.

"I do not wish to go to the Allen's tonight," he admitted as he stabbed his last piece of chicken with his fork.

"And why is that, my dear?"

"I would rather be at home," he said around his food. "Where there are no debutantes," he added after he had swallowed.

"Ah," his aunt said, knowingly. "You are still attempting to avoid your duty to marry."

"I am not avoiding it," he protested before taking a large gulp of his wine. These glasses were not big enough to hold the full amount of wine for which this conversation was likely going to make him wish. He did not fancy having a discussion of his shortcomings where Miss Bennet was concerned, nor did he relish the thought of having to yet again be reminded of his need for a wife.

"I fully intend to fulfill my duty to the family after I have seen Connie well-settled." And as soon as he could find a lady who was of interest.

He did not wish to marry just to fulfill a duty. He longed for a lady who would do more than provide him with children and be an excellent hostess. He desired companionship. Someone to whom he could talk even more freely than he could his sister and aunt. A lady who would understand and care for his heart and not just his home.

"Your sister has found her happy future," his aunt replied. "So, now, it is your turn." She held up a hand when Trefor opened his mouth to protest. "There is still plenty of time left in this season. I am not saying you must find a wife before summer. I am only suggesting you consider a few ladies."

Trefor drained what remained in his wine glass. "Connie is not yet married." And not a single lady which he had met so far this season had captured his interest in any particularly marriage-inspiring fashion.

His aunt merely raised her brows and pursed her lips in reply. She clearly did not approve of his reasoning. Not that she needed to approve of it. It was the only explanation he felt compelled to share. A declaration of "no lady has met my requirements" would only lead to a list being drawn up and an analysis of all the ladies which either his aunt or sister knew would begin. That was how his sister did things – scientifically. And his aunt would only happily join in for she was desperate to have grand-nieces and nephews.

"I will join you in the drawing room when it is time to leave." He sighed as he rose and paused a moment to look at Aunt Gwladys, "You truly wish to attend this reading?"

His aunt nodded. "I do. For if you will not look for a bride, then I must do it for you."

"You do not need to find a wife for me."

"I did not say I would find one," she replied with a mischievous smile. "I only said I was going to look for one. You, of course, will have the final decision."

"How gracious of you," he muttered before leaving the room and seeking out a haven of peace and quiet.

Discussions of marriage made him uneasy. He had always said that choosing a wife was a monumental responsibility – not that his good friends, Charles and Henry, had ever agreed with him until recently.

He bounded up the stairs as if fleeing from a monster that hunted him in a calculating fashion. There, of course, was no actual monster chasing him. It was only his fear that he would not choose correctly when selecting the companion of his future life.

However, the problem with imaginary monsters was the very real fact that one could not outrun them or hide from them. Not even sleep was effective against them, for even in dreams they were known to torment their victims. There simply was no escape.

He pushed open the door to his apartment. This sitting room had been a safe harbour for him since both his father and mother had died. Here, he found he could hear his mother's voice the most. His father's memories were tied much more closely with the study. That is where he would retreat to contemplate many decisions regarding the effective running of the estate. But here... He took off his jacket and tossed it on the sofa before sinking into his mother's favourite chair. Here he would seek his mother's guidance.

How many times had he sat here on her knee or peered over the arm of the chair as he stood beside it? Too many to be counted, but each had been indelibly engrained upon his heart. He could not accurately tell anyone what had been said or what events had occurred in all those times, but the feeling he had always had here was one of comfort and deep, abiding love.

What would his mother say if she were to hear that he had been rude to a lady – a very pretty lady with expressive hazel eyes and brown hair only a shade darker than the colour of his bay?

He did not need to ponder that for any length of time, for he knew precisely what she would say. He needed to apologize.

It would not matter to his mother that this particular young lady caused his chest to tighten and his thoughts to become tangled. She would take him by his chin, look into his eyes, and remind him that a gentleman always – without fail – corrected his errors. To ignore them was not honourable. Then, she would smile at him and kiss his forehead before sending him on his way to mend whatever needed fixing.

He expelled a great breath. How he was supposed to correct his error when his mind and mouth seemed at odds was beyond him, but he knew he must try.

So it was that later that evening, Trefor Linton entered the Allen's drawing room and immediately began his search for Miss Bennet.

"Are you looking for someone?" Charles Edward inquired.

"Miss Bennet," Trefor said, sparing a quick look for his friend. "Good evening, Miss Barrett," he greeted his friend's betrothed.

"Is there a reason you are looking for this lady?" Evelyn Barrett asked.

"My aunt wishes for an introduction." And Trefor was happy for the excuse it would give him to present himself as a proper gentleman to Miss Bennet and her relations.

Ah! There she was, wearing another blue dress, though this one was not as dark as the one she had worn earlier. This one looked a lot like the sky on a clear summer's day. He smiled.

"Found her, did you?" Charles whispered. There

was a teasing tone to his words which caused Trefor to scowl.

"I did, which means I can be done with my duty as quickly as possible." He turned to find his aunt, as well as his sister and Miss Barrett, speaking to Mrs. Allen. "Or perhaps not," he muttered. "What are you doing?"

Charles had lifted his hand as if waving to someone.

"Acknowledging the presence of Mr. Darcy. He was looking this direction. I did not wish to appear rude." His lips twitched, and his brows rose as he said the word rude.

"I was taken by surprise. I did not expect her to be entering the drawing room while I was exiting."

"Of course," Charles replied with the most obviously feigned serious look Trefor had ever seen.

He rolled his eyes and shook his head. Charles had always been incorrigible, and it did not seem that being on the precipice of marriage had changed that entirely. He still enjoyed being shocking and a general nuisance.

"Mr. Edwards."

Trefor swallowed as he turned to find Mr. Darcy had approached them. Hopefully, if the gentleman had heard about the incident at Mrs. Verity's, he would not censure him too severely for Trefor's behavior towards his wife's sister.

"Mrs. Darcy's sister told me that the tables have arrived. Have you seen them?" Darcy asked.

"Not yet," Charles replied, "but I am certain they are perfection if you have chosen them."

Darcy smiled and chuckled softly. "My wife chose them."

"Then I am certain they are far better than perfect," Charles replied with all the ease of a charmer.

"She would be happy to hear it," Darcy said. "And, you are most likely correct." He glanced at Trefor.

"Allow me to present my friend, Mr. Trefor Linton," Charles said. "Linton, this is Mr. Fitzwilliam Darcy."

"It is a pleasure to meet you." Pleasure was perhaps not the best word for what Trefor felt as Darcy gave him an appraising look.

"I am equally delighted to meet you." Darcy's lips twitched slightly. "I have heard a good deal about you."

Trefor groaned softly. "I had hoped to apologize

for that. I was not in the best frame of mind earlier today."

"He had no desire to be here tonight," Charles inserted, "but his aunt insisted he come."

Blasted Charles! Did he not know when teasing was most unwelcomed? That bit did not need to be shared!

"My plans had been changed, which meant I needed to collect my sister from Verity House sooner than expected," Trefor explained. It still sounded as sorry now as it had earlier at supper when he had attempted to explain his offending Miss Bennet to his aunt. Such an admission, Trefor was certain, was not going to gain him any favour in Mr. Darcy's opinion.

However, to Trefor's surprise, Darcy chuckled.

"A foul temper can lead to some grave errors," the man said with a knowing smile. "There are chairs near us. How many are in your party?"

"Counting Edwards and Miss Barrett, we are six."

"I think we can accommodate that many," Darcy assured him.

Gaining his aunt's attention, Trefor made quick work of introducing her, as well as his sister and

Mr. Crawford, who had joined them by that time, to Mr. Darcy before following the gentleman across the room and going through the formalities of introductions once again. Then, Trefor was obliged to sit beside his aunt who had claimed the seat nearest Miss Bennet and Miss Darcy.

"Are you reading tonight?" Aunt Gwladys asked Miss Bennet, who smiled and shook her head.

"I have only just arrived in town," she explained. "I am certain I do not know enough people yet to be invited to do such a thing."

"But you would like to?" Trefor asked. It sounded to him as if she was disappointed that she could not read tonight. He, on the other hand, was content to sit and listen.

"I enjoy reading," she replied. "Does that sur‐prise you?" She pressed her lips together as if embarrassed for having been direct, just as she had done this afternoon.

"I suppose it does," he answered. "Although, it is likely not for the reason you assume."

"And what reason might you have then?" his aunt asked.

"Performing in front of strangers would be uncomfortable to me, so it is hard to imagine it would not be for everyone." He shrugged. "It is perhaps not a good answer, but there it is."

Miss Bennet leaned towards his aunt, and by extension him. "I would not be performing for strangers."

"You would not be?" She knew no one in attendance. Even if she knew the host well enough to be asked, she would still not know each of the twenty or so people who sat on the tufted chairs and patterned sofas in the Allen's drawing room.

"No. I would read to my sister."

"But what of the other people?"

She shrugged. "It matters little if they listen to me read to Elizabeth or not, for I would only wish to please my sister."

His brows rose. "That is a different way of looking at an experience."

"But you do not approve."

"No, no," he said quickly. He had most certainly left her with a very sorry opinion of himself. "I think it is quite a good idea actually."

"Then you would not mind reading to me?" his aunt asked.

"What have you done?" he attempted to keep the growl he felt out of his tone of voice.

"Mrs. Allen asked if you would read. It seems one of the gentlemen who was supposed to read this evening has fallen ill, and she was in as desperate state to find a replacement."

"Aunt."

"I know how willing you are to lend assistance." The innocent smile she gave him was anything but. She was up to something.

"And you promised her I would do it?"

His aunt's eyes fluttered in response.

He sighed. "When will I get the piece I am to read? You knew I would not disappoint you, did you not?"

His aunt's hand covered his. "You are such a good boy. Mrs. Allen will be over with it in just a moment." She looked across the room to their hostess and gave a nod.

Miss Bennet's eyes were dancing with amusement.

"Do you know what I am to read? Or when?"

"You are starting us off."

"First? I must read first?"

"Yes, the evening is a selection of excerpts from novels..."

"It is not a poetry reading?"

His aunt shook her head.

"Novels?"

"Yes, dear. Those dreadful things."

He rolled his eyes.

"Do you not approve of novels, Mr. Linton?" Miss Bennet's seemed both shocked and horrified by such a thought.

"I cannot say I read them often, but I am not opposed to them. It is just that I was under the impression that we would be hearing poetry tonight. I rather enjoy poetry."

"Did I not say literary reading?"

His aunt was once again attempting to look innocent. She needed to work on the expression if she wished to be believable.

"No, you said it was, and I quote, 'a poetry or some such thing reading.'"

"Well, then I was not wrong," she said with a sly smile. "You will read a poem to introduce our topic for the evening." She took a paper from Mrs. Allen and handed it to him.

"When you are ready," Mrs. Allen said. "I am going to welcome everyone, and then you can read that."

"Just read it to me," his aunt whispered.

Trefor nodded and rose from his place.

"He is such a good boy," he heard her say to Miss Bennet.

He looked over the poem that was written in neat close letters. It did not seem a difficult piece to read. Still, his heart beat a rather loud and rapid beat as he listened to Mrs. Allen greet her guests and explain how the evening was to proceed before introducing him.

Trefor took a deep breath and looked at his aunt whose smile reminded him a great deal of his mother's. Reading to her would not be a trial.

"'A Receipt for Writing a Novel' by Mrs. Alcock. *Would you a favourite novel make*," he looked up from his page and caught the look of delight on Miss Bennet's face. Glancing down again at the paper he held, he paused, attempting to find where he had left off. "Forgive me," he muttered. "Let me begin again."

He would read to the paper and only the paper. For looking in his aunt's direction would mean seeing Miss Bennet and, even with words written for him to simply utter, she seemed able to confuse the communication between his mind and his mouth.

With his eyes firmly focused on the paper he began once more.

"*Would you a favourite novel make,*

Try hard your reader's heart to break

For who is pleased, if not tormented?

(Novels for that were first invented.)"[1]

As were poetry readings and pretty ladies with expressive hazel eyes, he thought before reading on.

1. *A Receipt for Writing a Novel,* Mary Alcock.

Chapter 6

"Was is not a lovely evening?" Kitty asked with a sigh as she waited to leave the Allen's home. Those who had been in attendance were milling about the room, stopping to chat with one another, as Mr. Darcy and Mr. Edwards were doing right now, and then, slowly moving toward the door to thank their hostess before taking their leave.

"I thoroughly enjoyed it," Georgiana Darcy answered.

"As did I," Miss Linton agreed. "The way each excerpt from the various novels was highlighted using the bits and pieces of the poem that started us off was brilliant."

"It was a very clever way to present it," Kitty's sister, Elizabeth added. The ladies of their party save for Miss Barrett, who was with Mr. Edwards, and Miss Linton's aunt, who was speaking to another lady, were all standing together.

"Well, I am just glad it is over." Mr. Linton was looking over their heads toward the door.

Why could he not be with Mr. Darcy and Mr. Edwards instead of standing watch over his sister and Mr. Crawford?

"You did not like it?" Kitty asked.

"I apologize. Who did not like what?" Mr. Linton asked.

Kitty blinked. Had he not heard himself?

"You said you were glad it was over," his sister whispered.

"I said that?" His eyes grew wide.

"You most certainly did," Mr. Crawford assured him as Kitty nodded along with his sister and the rest of her companions.

"That was supposed to be a thought," he admitted sheepishly. "It is not that I did not enjoy the reading. I am just anxious to be home."

To Kitty, it did not appear, from the way he diverted his gaze from his group to the door, that he was being completely honest. She firmly believed he was anxious to be home. However she suspected that his desire to be home was most

likely due to his longing to be gone from her presence – she was, after all, a tradesman's niece. She
rolled her eyes as she thought the bitter words. It
really was too bad Mr. Linton was so pompous in
his opinions, for he was rather handsome in his
wine-coloured jacket and cream breeches. He had,
in her opinion, been the most handsome gentleman in attendance. Well, other than his friend Mr.
Edwards, that is.

"Who was the gentleman sitting across the room
on the green chair?" Kitty whispered to her sister.
That gentleman had also been quite attractive in
his black jacket and red waistcoat. His hair was
not much darker than Mr. Linton's, and he was
likely shorter and less broad than Mr. Linton, but
he seemed more willing to smile than scowl, which
was very pleasantly unlike Mr. Linton.

"I am certain I could not tell you," Elizabeth
answered. "I am not as familiar with everyone as I
would like to be."

Kitty sighed. That was the trouble with having a
sister so newly married. Elizabeth was very good at
meeting people and remembering names, but she
had only been in town for a few months. Therefore, she had not had enough time to meet all the

truly interesting people about whom Kitty wondered – such as that handsome gentleman on the green chair.

"Mr. Hayes," Mr. Linton answered.

"Were you listening to me speak to my sister?" Kitty asked with no little amount of agitation. How rude! If one were to listen to whispers, one should not let the source of the whisper know that he had intruded on a private conversation. That was why one whispered in public, after all. What was said in a low tone was not meant to be heard by everyone. Surely, that fact was just as true in London as it was in Meryton.

"I did not mean to listen," he apologized.

At least, he knew he was in the wrong. That was a point in his favour.

"I just happened to hear and knew the answer. Was there a particular reason you wished to know who Mr. Hayes is?"

"Yes."

"And what was that?"

He expected her to tell him that? Kitty thought not! And she was certain her expression said so quite nicely since Mr. Linton's brow furrowed.

"Why do you suppose?" Miss Linton gave her brother a pointed glare.

Mr. Linton shook his head for a moment until realization washed over his features. "He is a bit of a fop," he muttered.

"If you mean he appears pleasant, as well as handsome, then I would have to agree," Kitty said, fixing her gaze on Mr. Linton's lovely blue eyes. They were silvery and strong. It really was a pity he was not more civil.

Mr. Crawford coughed, which was likely to cover a chuckle for he looked rather amused. Of course, Kitty did not see anything amusing about such rudeness, but then, she was not a rake. Perhaps rakes found things more humorous than the regular person.

"However," she continued, "if you are only attempting to disparage him to me, I should like to know why."

"Kitty," Elizabeth cautioned.

She should listen to Elizabeth. She knew she should. This was not a particularly good path down which to traverse, but the challenge had been put forth. Therefore, she stood her ground and ignored Elizabeth. She would be improper for just this moment – only long enough to have her point carried that Mr. Linton was being arrogant.

"I will give you that he's handsome," Mr. Linton replied. "But even he would tell you that. And he would likely do it just before he informed you which tailor he used and where to find the best muslin for your dress."

"What is wrong with my dress?" Kitty retorted.

"Not a thing." Mr. Linton looked to his sister for help. However, when none was forthcoming, he continued on by himself, which, as it turned out, was not the right choice. "It is a fine dress, but Mr. Hayes would likely comment on some small detail such as the fact that it will not survive many washings or that it would look better with a different lace on the sleeves."

Kitty's right hand flew to her left sleeve. "This is my favourite lace! And the fabric used for this dress is not catchpenny!"

"I did not say it was." Mr. Linton ran a finger around his collar. "And I can see why you like that lace, it is very nice."

"Nice? Only nice?" Kitty looked at her sleeve. This lace was so delicate that it spoke to a high degree of craftsmanship to create it, and he called it simply nice?

Mr. Crawford was coughing again, which made Mr. Linton glare at him.

"What would you have me call it?" he retorted sharply.

"Something better than nice," Kitty grumbled.

Mr. Linton blew out a breath as they came close enough to the door to feel the coolness of the night. "I was only imagining the sorts of things that Mr. Hayes might say. I was not saying any of that myself."

Kitty accepted her pelisse from a footman. "You sounded very much like an expert."

"That is because I have heard Hayes say such things before," Mr. Linton said, but Kitty paid no attention to him other than to listen and peek at him from the corner of her eye.

"You will still call on me despite my brother?" Miss Linton looked apologetic as she asked.

"Of course," Kitty assured her. "You cannot control your brother any more than I can stop my sister Mary from scolding and lecturing, and I should very much dislike it if I were not to have friends because of her." She pressed her lips together. "That was not kind. I should not speak so about my sister."

Thankfully, Miss Linton smiled at Kitty before turning to thank their hostess for the wonderful evening.

"I like her," Kitty whispered.

"She does seem very pleasant," Georgiana agreed. "And her brother is handsome."

"And boorish." Kitty grimaced. That was not kind, even if it was true. Why could she not behave properly? She glared at the back of Mr. Linton. It was his fault. She had been doing so well until he knocked that tin out of her hands at Mrs. Verity's.

"I think you might be judging him too harshly," Elizabeth said.

A scowl settled on Kitty's face. She did not need her sister to reprimand her. Just because Mr. Darcy had proven to not be so bad-mannered as he had appeared at first, did not mean that all such rudeness was to be readily forgiven. Mr. Linton had thought she was a maid! And when she was wearing her best blue day dress! The one which had only been completed before she left Longbourn for town. Not even her friends at home had seen it. And he – the handsome, frustrating gentleman who read poetry very well – had thought it was no better than what a maid might wear. She pulled her eyes from him and back to her sister and Miss Darcy as first one and then the other thanked Mrs. Allen for the evening.

"I had a lovely time," Kitty said to Mrs. Allen when it was her turn.

"It was a pleasure to meet you, Miss Bennet," their hostess replied. "I do hope we will cross paths at another soiree."

Kitty thanked her and followed her sister and Mr. Darcy out of the house, down the steps, and to their waiting carriage. As she settled into her seat, she knew what she would be writing in her notebook.

~*~*~

After describing her night to her aunt as she readied herself for bed, Kitty settled into the chair next to the small desk in her room and opened her notebook. She was not yet ready for sleep, but a few moments of writing might put the enjoyment and frustration of the evening out of her mind and prepare her for her repose.

Picking up her pen and thinking back to the man

with the ragged coat she and her uncle had seen earlier in the day, she began.

> *The education of Mr. L-, who was cursed for his behavior and doomed to trudge the earth while wearing his character on his back*

She smiled. That was a good title. A bit longish, but quite descriptive.

> *The hall was dank and dingy. The walls were thick, dotted here and there with windows entirely too small for the vastness of the room. There was an enormous fireplace at one end. Large enough for two servants to stand inside when the fires were not lit, which only happened when their master was away. Try as they might maids and footmen attempted to keep it and the whole of the hall clean with the meager supplies their master provided, but the task was impossible. He was a miserly old goat. His coffers were not lacking for gold, but his heart possessed barely a morsel of sense or compassion.*
>
> *In the midst of this stony portrait was a man, who had once been nearly as feelingless and hardened as the master of this great estate. This man, this Mr. L, was a relatively new arrival at the*

mansion, sent there by the princess of the land, whom Mr. L had failed to recognize with the honour she was due.

Today, as every day, Mr. L stood at the ready to fetch whatever his master required, be it his account books, a glass of wine, a piece of bread, or even a chamber pot

Mr. L's coat dragged along the dusty floor of the great hall as he carried an empty basket, which had been filled with warm rolls, to the sideboard. His coat was a ragged old thing, though once it had been a fine blue greatcoat made of the best material that could be purchased in the land. He could not remove it. The curse under which he had fallen would not allow it, and with each passing day, the wretched old coat seemed to grow longer and more tattered. And with each tear and with each time he stumbled over the hem, Mr. L longed to have his old coat back – not to mention his comfortable bed and warm fire, as well as his own servants.

"You!"

Mr. L jumped at the bark of his master.

"Get me more wine!"

More wine was never a good thing. Mr. L knew

that very well. Each glass made his master more and more belligerent. However, not bringing the required wine would not make his master any more friendly either. So, Mr. L wisely hurried from the room to retrieve the desired beverage.

Perhaps if he was quick enough, he might return before he noticed the cold of the ground through his worn shoes. The floors of the manor house were dirty and hard and not at all like the fine house in which he had once lived, but, at least, they were warm.

Kitty paused and read over the few lines she had written. Smiling, she picked up her pen again.

"Mr. L," a boy called to him, "my mother needs a log for her fire, and I cannot get it."

The man stopped, eying the young lad. The boy did not look frail or terribly undersized. Indeed, he looked quite capable of fetching a log or two. "I must return with the wine," he said. "My master will not be pleased if I delay."

"But my mother is not well," the boy pleaded.

"I cannot," Mr. L said, but upon turning away, his coat, in response to his refusal, tore at the elbow.

With a sigh, he turned back. "Which log?"

He did not have time for this quest, but he also did not wish for any more holes in his coat. There were far too many already that let in the damp, chilled air of this gloomy place.

"The one beside the great tree in the grove of ancient trees. It will burn longer and warmer than any other, and such heat will surely heal my mother."

"The great tree?" That was a far distance out of the way.

"Please, Mr. L. My mother is ill."

The man's jacket hung heavily on him, pulling him down. "Could you go to the winemaker for me while I am gone?"

"I cannot leave my mother," the young lad said.

You must show kindness of the greatest kind. The words whispered through Mr. L's mind reminding him of his duty, of the only way he could ever be free of this torn cloak.

"I will get the log," he assured the boy. "See to your mother."

Again, Kitty paused. Her page was nearly filled. A yawn crept over her. Tilting her head from side to side, she attempted to drive the fatigue away, but as another yawn told her, it was no use. Sleep would not be put off for much longer. It had been a long and busy day, and her bed was calling to her. Her body longed for its repose. Reluctantly, she put her pen away and rose from the small desk.

Taking her lamp with her, she crossed to the bed where she placed the lamp on the bedside table. Then, she took off her robe, slipped her feet out of her slippers, and climbed under the covers, sighing into the mattress for a moment before sitting up once again and putting out her lamp.

In the dark, she wiggled deep into her blankets, wrapping them around her shoulders and scuffing her feet against the sheets to help the bedding warm faster.

Once again, she yawned. She would not have to ponder which dream she would like to have tonight, for tonight, she hoped to see Mr. Linton in his ragged, old coat scurrying across a field and over a hill to the ancient old forest as his punishing quest to learn to be kind began.

Chapter 7

The day after the literary reading dawned with a thin layer of fog obscuring the brightness of the morning, but that did not stop Trefor from requesting that his bay be saddled so that he could ride. The feeling that left was right and up was down which had settled on him yesterday afternoon at Mrs. Verity's house had not shifted. It seemed that neither whisky nor sleep could drive it from him, and no amount of scolding from his sister or his aunt – and there had been a fair amount of that – could purge his mind of its jumbled state. Therefore, he hoped that beginning his day as he would any other day would set him on a path to having his well-ordered mind and life set back to right.

However, even eating the exact breakfast he ate every day, while reading the paper in the same order in which he always read it, did not seem to be having the desired effect. Perplexed and a great deal more than a little annoyed, he went to his study to push around a few account books and deal with some correspondence. There was an estate matter about which his steward had written him that needed addressing, and then, he would have to go through the invitations that he and his sister had received to decide which ones he would willingly attend with his aunt.

He knew that Aunt Gwladys would wish to accept them all until she had succeeded in seeing not only his sister, but also him, happily betrothed. However, there was a limit to his tolerance for his aunt's encouragement which was growing smaller and smaller as the season progressed.

That was how it was each year. The season would start with great anticipation. The soirees were a welcome diversion, but then, come March or April, the diversions would begin to grow dull, and he would start longing to be home where he could make himself useful on his estate. As a consequence, when the season would draw to a close, Trefor would be relieved to be packing up house and travelling home.

He poured himself a glass of whisky. It was not his normal wont to consume such a drink while working on his accounts. He usually reserved this particular drink for when the sun had set and he was entertaining himself with a book or partaking in a discussion with his sister and aunt before retiring for the night.

Today, however, he was making an exception to that regular pattern because his books were balanced, his letter had been written, and the stack of invitations had been whittled to an acceptable amount, and yet, he did not feel as he should. Something was off, and so he was willing to take pleasure in a favourite drink while... he shook his head, chuckled, and did what was most certainly out of the ordinary for him — he waited.

He had left the study door open a crack so that the sound of any callers would reach him. He shook his head again. The partially opened door was only more evidence that all was not as it had always been in his world, for he was not waiting for just any callers to arrive. Miss Bennet was to call on his sister today, and he was determined to once again attempt to prove to her that he could behave appropriately even if she did seem eager to misconstrue every word he uttered.

He was just finishing the last of his whisky when he heard that for which he had been waiting. The front door opened, followed by feminine voices wafting down the corridor to his study. Miss Bennet and her sister, Mrs. Darcy, were here.

Trefor remained seated, counting out a minute and a half before he rose. Then, after depositing his glass on his desk in a slow and deliberate fashion, he made his way to the sitting room.

"Crawford," he greeted his friend who was in the entryway. "I assume you are here to see my sister."

"Indeed, I am, although a game of billiards would not be unwelcome if she is occupied."

Trefor's brow furrowed. His sister did have callers – callers whom he wished to see, or more precisely one in particular whom he did not want to miss seeing for at least a few minutes.

"I think Connie would like to see you first," he suggested.

Henry's brows rose. "But I can hear she has guests."

"There is no harm in saying *good day* before we play, is there?"

"She is not entertaining gentlemen, so why are you so eager to join her?"

That was a good question but not one which Trefor felt prepared to answer. In fact, he was convinced it was a question which would prove impossible to answer should he wish to attempt it, which he did not.

"I am not eager. It is just that I have walked from my study to here, so it seems pointless for me to retrace those steps only to have to return to the sitting room later."

"That makes little sense," Henry muttered.

Trefor shrugged and nodded for the sitting room door to be opened. His reasoning seemed to make sense to him, which should perhaps concern him considering the higgledy-piggledy state of his mind. He motioned for Henry to enter before him. That way he could take in the arrangement of the ladies in the room without it being obvious to his friend.

"You are joining us?" his aunt asked when she saw him.

"I like tea," he replied.

She lifted a questioning brow.

"It is not as if I do not join you on occasion."

"No," she agreed, "but I do find it curious."

"I have a few invitations for you to consider." He ignored her curiosity and gave her the stack he held.

"And were there others?" she asked as he took a seat nearer to where Miss Bennet sat.

"There were, but I thought we would start with those," he replied.

"I am constantly amazed at how many invitations my husband receives," Mrs. Darcy said. "There is just no way we can attend everything, and to be honest, Mr. Darcy is not overly fond of being away from home night after night."

"I can understand that," Trefor said. "I do not find the soirees unpleasant, but there is comfort in being home and quiet now and again."

"And certain soirees are more agreeable than others," Henry added with a smile. "Though I do find I enjoy attending soirees much more than I enjoy being at home. That is likely due to who will be there." He smiled at Constance, who responded in kind.

"Yes," she agreed, "I have developed a fondness

for them myself that I never had before I was betrothed."

Miss Bennet sighed as if what his sister said was the most wonderful thing she had ever heard. A romantic. Miss Bennet must be a romantic. That was not something he had ever been. He was more practical and not so flighty as a romantic person was prone to be.

"I find Mr. Darcy enjoys soirees more now that we are married than he did before we were married." Mrs. Darcy shared a secret smile with her sister.

"Oh, yes!" Miss Bennet said with some feeling. "He was positively miserable at the assembly in Meryton." She turned to Constance. "That is where we first met him. He was a guest at Netherfield. That is the estate next to my fathers which Mr. Bingley – Mr. Darcy's particular friend and now my sister Jane's husband – has taken. It is a beautiful home, and the gardens are so inviting."

It was a bit of a wandering way to say something, but there was such animation to Miss Bennet's features when she spoke that Trefor found he did not mind the nomadic path her speech had taken.

"It is a happy thing for your sister to be settled

so close to home," he said, attempting to enter the conversation in a way that would not be offensive.

"I think Mama would agree," Miss Bennet replied. "However, I do not expect it to remain as it is."

"You do not?" Mrs. Darcy sounded surprised.

Miss Bennet placed a hand on her sister's. "Jane loves you, and Mr. Bingley will not wish to be separated from his friend. They will find another place to call home soon after you and Mr. Darcy leave for Pemberley."

"But what of your mother?" Trefor asked, genuinely curious to know.

Miss Bennet laughed lightly. "She will not be without company. There are Mary, Lydia, and me, not to mention Mrs. Philips – that is Mama's sister – and Lady Lucas, who is Mama's particular friend." Her brow furrowed as her lips pursed in a most becoming expression of thought. "There are also several other ladies who come to call and all the tenants on whom to call." She emitted a small sigh. "But once my other sisters and I marry, she will have no one to accompany her on those calls."

"You accompany her?" Trefor asked.

"Oh, yes! It is very enjoyable."

"It is?"

"Yes."

Her brow was beginning to furrow. He needed to say something that would not cause that crease between her eyes to deepen.

"What is it about the visits that you like?"

She blinked her eyes as if he was asking something that should be obvious.

"The people," was her simple answer.

"I promise I am not being obtuse," he began, "but what about the people makes the task so agreeable?" He truly wished to understand her thinking and hoped she understood that.

"Well," she said before expelling a breath as if answering was a bit of a chore, but not a disagreeable one. "I find that calls such as this one and the ones in the tenant's homes fill me with..." Her voice trailed off as her features took on that becoming expression she seemed to favor when thinking.

"Lightness?" Constance suggested.

"Yes! That would be one way to say it. And if there are children who need attention," she shrugged, "I do like to read aloud." She blinked and drew a quick breath. "Perhaps that is why you do not understand it."

"Understand what?" he asked cautiously.

"My liking to visit the tenants. You said you did not like to read aloud last night, so could it not be that my enjoying chatting and reading to children seems foreign to you since you would not like it?" She tipped her head and looked at him expectantly.

"I honestly have not attempted to call on the wives of my tenants or read to their children. My mother always did that, and then Connie did it after Mother died."

"Then it seems you will either need to learn how or find a wife," Miss Bennet said in all seriousness before her eyes grew wide with horror. "Not that I am putting myself forward. We would never suit, but if you cannot visit the tenants, you must find someone who can." She ducked her head. "I was doing so well," she muttered.

He was not certain what she was no longer doing well, but her embarrassment caused him to want to say something that would ease it. Of course, he could not think of a single thing, and, therefore, he was not at all put out when his aunt took up the conversation.

"I have told him that he needs to find a wife, and

I welcome your support on the matter, Miss Bennet." She smiled kindly at Miss Bennet. "Finding a wife to suit him has been a bit of a challenge. This is not his first season."

Miss Bennet giggled softly at that.

"I have discriminating tastes," he muttered as he was positive his aunt would expect some form of protest.

"We could make a list of what you are looking for in a wife," Henry said with a smirk.

Trefor shook his head. "That might have worked for you, but I prefer not to create a list of ladies and check them off one by one."

"You did that?" Miss Bennet asked Henry in utter shock.

Henry nodded. "I was attempting to reform my former behavior."

"Of course," Miss Bennet said, "you were a rake or some such thing."

"Kitty," Mrs. Darcy scolded softly.

Miss Bennet sighed and apologized.

"I am not offended. I was not what I should have been, and Miss Linton was gracious enough to help me learn to be a proper gentleman."

"And then I created a list of ladies for him."

Miss Bennet looked like she was going to faint away. "No! You did?"

Constance nodded. "It broke my heart to do it, but I had promised I would."

Miss Bennet's hand covered her heart as she shook her head. "How tragic."

"There are several interesting bits to that tale, which I will tell you when we are not beset on every side by gentlemen," Constance assured her. "Suffice it to say that none of the ladies on that list met with Mr. Crawford's approval, and I was fortunate to gain his favour."

Again, the romantic Miss Bennet sighed wistfully. But then, she sat up a little straighter, her eyes shining with excitement.

"Then, perhaps you could help me."

"With what?" Trefor asked before he could think better of it.

"With behaving as I ought while in town. It is not that I am an improper lady like Mr. Crawford was an improper gentleman. I just have never been to town before, and, well, I would like to make a good impression. After all, I would like to marry someday, and, to be frank, there are not many gentlemen from whom to choose in Hertfordshire – at least, there are none to my liking," she clarified.

"If Miss Linton helped me, perhaps her brother could help you by giving you a gentleman's viewpoint," Mr. Crawford suggested.

Miss Bennet shook her head vigorously. "That would not work."

Trefor was inclined to agree. He had seen what had happened when he had allowed his sister to help Henry.

"I am certain I need a lady's advice," Miss Bennet continued as Trefor recalled the article in the paper with his sister's name attached to it.

"Besides, Mr. Linton is far too provoking," she concluded, bringing Trefor's full attention back to the discussion at hand.

"I am provoking?" he asked incredulously.

"Yes."

"I do not see how."

Her brow furrowed as a scowl settle on her lips. "Must you always argue with me?"

"I do not argue with you. You argue with me," he retorted. Blast! That was not what he should have said. It was not what he would have said to any other lady, other than his sister.

Miss Bennet rolled her eyes and while making a sweeping motion with her hand towards him, said to Constance, "You see what I mean?"

Constance laughed. "Yes, I know very well of what you speak. He provokes me regularly, but he means well – most of the time."

"If you say so," Miss Bennet replied, though she did not sound at all convinced of the fact.

It was probably best that he leave now before he made things worse. "Crawford, if you are still interested in billiard, I would not be averse to a game or two." He rose, and thankfully, Henry joined him. However, before he left the room, there was one thing he needed to do.

He turned to Miss Bennet. "I am pleased that you and your sister were able to call on my sister and aunt today. I think Connie would do well to have friends such as you and Mrs. Darcy." He paused. "And, your dress is very pretty. Lavender suits you very well." He smiled at her look of sur-prise. "It is not at all maid-like nor is it in anyway pinchpenny. I know it cannot completely atone for my poor behaviour yesterday, but I do hope it is a start."

She blinked at him as if she was uncertain what

to say. "Yes," she managed after a moment, "it is a very good start."

A feeling of accomplishment settled on Trefor as he quit the room. He had nearly managed to do what he had planned. Had it not been for that small disagreement, that would have been an excellent meeting with Miss Bennet. As it was, it was the best they had had so far, and that was promising. What exactly it promised he was not certain. He was just glad that this time when he left her, he did not do so feeling as low as an ant carrying an apple.

Chapter 8

Candles set high on candelabras stood at both the near and far ends of the ballroom while a chandelier glowed from above. The musicians were tucked neatly into a corner near the far end of the ballroom as the hopeful dancers formed the first set.

Kitty was happy to not be part of this first set. She would much rather sit along the wall and watch her sister and Mr. Darcy while allowing her heart to slow its pace and become acquainted with her setting. A ball was thrilling to be sure and even knowing few in attendance could not dampen the excitement she felt.

She smiled at the gentleman, who was watching her across the room, before quickly turning her eyes in the opposite direction. She should not have even encouraged him with a smile. She was to wait to be properly introduced to anyone she did not already know before accepting a dance partner. Yet, smiling had seemed the most natural thing in all the world to do, for it was what she would have done at any assembly in Meryton.

"The décor is just what it should be," the voice of a welcome companion pulled her from her observation of the ballroom.

"Indeed, it is, Mrs. Kendrick," Kitty agreed as Mr. Linton and his aunt joined her.

"You should be dancing," Mrs. Kendrick said.

"Oh, I will. I am sure I will not have to sit for more than this first dance," Kitty assured Mrs. Kendrick while purposefully not looking at Mr. Linton.

He was wearing a blue jacket tonight with a grey waistcoat and matching breeches. If a combination of colours could be chosen to make his eyes appear to best advantage, blue and grey was it. And while admiring the way his clothing set off his eyes would be excessively agreeable, Kitty did not need to be further confused by him than she already was.

Yesterday, he had been rude – abominably so, in her opinion. But then, today, he had been nearly charming. She ran her thumb across the edge of her folded fan. If he had been as pleasant yesterday as he had been today, she would not have written him into her story as a cursed gentleman.

What would she write tonight? A curse was not just lifted with one stroke of the pen until several trials had been completed. She knew she would have to torture him in some way in her story. However, his attractive attire and smile were not going to make it easy for her to do. Therefore, ignoring him as much as possible was the best course of action.

"My sister informs me that I am to request the second dance of the evening," Mr. Linton said, interrupting her thoughts.

Of course, he was not going to make ignoring him an easy task.

"I would not wish to inconvenience you," she replied with a tight smile. Being asked to dance just to appease a sister's desire was not precisely flattering.

Mr. Linton face was furrowed with confusion. "It is no inconvenience," he said in a cautious tone with a questioning lilt at the end.

"What Trefor is attempting to say is that his sister reminded him of his desire to dance with you," Mrs. Kendrick said.

"That is not precisely what I was attempting to say," he muttered, the look of confusion still on his face.

"Then, what, pray tell, were you saying?" his aunt asked.

The confused furrow between his eyes deepened as he took a seat next to his aunt. "I am not certain I can say without causing greater offense." Again, his statement ended with a questioning lilt.

"I am certain that Miss Bennet can withhold judgment until you have said all you need to say."

"Of course, I can," Kitty agreed.

"I did not mean to say that she could not."

Mr. Linton was looking positively ill, which was odd.

"My sister told me how she had mentioned to you, Miss Bennet, that I would be willing to ask you to dance – which I am." He blew out a breath. "By the by, you look exquisite tonight. The ribbon winding through your curls is very nice."

His eyes seemed to fixate on her head which caused her to touch her hair without thought to make sure all was well with it. Nothing seemed out of place.

"Then, as I was entering the carriage tonight,

Connie reminded me that I was to ask for a dance and suggested that the second dance would be best as we were going to be too late for the first dance and having a partner for one of the beginning dances would set you up well for the evening. If you can get one sheep to enter the pasture, the others will often follow."

"Sheep?"

"Yes, yes, I will be the first to dance with you and then the others will follow."

His eyes had left her hair and were now following the dancers on the floor.

"Do you think I am incapable of acquiring a partner without your help?"

His head snapped back towards her. "Is that what I said?"

"It did sound that way," his aunt answered.

"That is not at all what I meant."

Kitty waited for his explanation while he studied first the room and then her.

"You are beautiful, as any gentleman here can see, and you will not lack for partners. However, according to Crawford and my sister, a desirable young woman becomes more so when she has ample admirers. So, I am just to help guarantee that a lady worthy of admiration receives all that she is due."

Kitty could not help but smile and blush at such words. When he was not stumbling over his words, Mr. Linton was capable of being rather worthy of swooning.

"And that is just like the sheep. If one of them can be persuaded to enter the field and eat the fresh grass and flowers, then the others will follow."

And then, he was back to stumbling. Her brow furrowed. She did not want to be fresh grass.

"Not that anyone needs to be persuaded to dance with you." He shook his head.

"It might be best if you stop trying to explain your odd metaphor," his aunt said. "Trefor is fond of strange saying. You are not a field that needs to be eaten to the ground by sheep. It is that sometimes gentlemen need leading." She smiled at her nephew who scowled in reply.

"I am not in need of leading," he muttered.

What was it that Mama had said a gentleman sometimes wanted? "Encouragement." That was it!

"I beg your pardon?" Mr. Linton said.

"It is not that gentlemen need leading," Kitty explained. "They need encouragement."

"I do like that idea better, but it does seem to be rather the same thing," Mr. Linton said in the same disgruntled tone he had used when protesting his aunt's words about needing to be led.

"The first set is half done," his aunt cautioned.

Mr. Linton took note of the dancers taking their places for the second half of the set. "Will you dance with me for the next set?" he asked Kitty. "I would be pleased if you did."

"Yes," Kitty answered. No one else had approached her yet – likely because Mr. Darcy was dancing. There was something about Mr. Darcy that caused other gentlemen to approach cautiously. Perhaps they had not yet learned that Mr. Darcy was not so dour as he appeared.

"You will?"

"Why are you surprised?" No gentleman had ever questioned an acceptance before.

He shrugged. "I do not know. I suppose I expected you to make me wait until the third or fourth set to prove you did not need my help in securing a partner or some such thing."

Kitty laughed. "I wish I had thought of that. My

sister Lydia likely would have. She is the best at scheming." Lydia knew precisely how to draw a gentleman along.

"Are the two of you close?" Mrs. Kendrick inquired.

"We are. Lydia is not quite two years younger than me, and we have always been friends."

"But you seem incapable of scheming." Mr. Linton watched the dancers as he spoke.

Was he questioning her intelligence?

His eyes grew wide as he glanced her direction. Her face must be speaking of her displeasure at being thought stupid.

"I meant that you seem too sincere to be a schemer. It was a compliment." His brows furrowed. "Not that I am criticizing your sister in any fashion either," he added before sighing. "It is a pity that conversation is necessary at these soirees, for I seem to be lacking the skill necessary to acquit myself as a polite gentleman." He shook his head. "I am not generally so offensive."

"He is not," his aunt agreed. "Unless, of course, you are Mr. Edwards or Mr. Crawford and in need of a reprimand. Then, Trefor would be the first to point out the error of your ways."

Kitty could tell from the smile that Mrs. Kendrick wore that she truly loved her nephew, and if a lady like Mrs. Kendrick, whom Kitty had decided she admired shortly after they had met this morning, loved Mr. Linton then he was likely not always as he appeared.

She sighed silently. That was not going to make it any easier to torture him on his quest to get the log from the great tree.

Her eyes swept the room, taking note of various dresses and coats, as well as a few fine-feathered hats.

"Who is that gentleman standing close to the musicians?" Kitty asked. "He has been watching me, and I must admit he is rather handsome if a bit shorter than I would like."

"Mr. Densmore," Trefor replied. "He is upstanding, but his estate could use some work — or so I hear. So if you have a good dowry, securing him would not be too challenging."

Kitty leaned toward Mrs. Kendrick. "Does Mr. Linton always give his opinion of gentlemen so freely to ladies?"

Mrs. Kendrick chuckled. "No. Other than his

sister, I believe you are the only lady who has ever been given such advice."

"It is very odd," Kitty whispered. "Not that it is unwelcomed intelligence, mind you."

"Do you have a substantial dowry?" Mrs. Kendrick asked in a whisper.

Kitty shook her head.

"But you are Mr. Darcy's sister now, so that will make some think that you might have a hefty purse," Mrs. Kendrick continued.

Well, that was most certainly unwelcome news. "Do you think Mr. Linton could tell me which ones are fortune hunters so that I do not hope where there is none?"

"Gladly," Mr. Linton whispered. "However, I would hold up my fan while having such a conversation to keep the interested from attempting to decipher what is being said."

There was so much to remember here in town! Kitty opened her fan and held it up.

"Thank you," she whispered.

"Anything to be of service, Miss Bennet," he replied with a relaxed smile.

Until this point, she had not seen him smile so easily, and what a beautiful smile it was, tipping up higher on the right than on the left while the sincerity of his words shone in his eyes.

"Ah, we have only a few more patterns, and then, it is our turn, Miss Bennet."

"Do you dance as well as you converse?" Kitty teased.

Mr. Linton chuckled. "Usually, yes, but then, usually I am not bumbling my words as I seem to do when I am with you." He glanced down at her feet. "I do hope your toes survive."

Kitty laughed. "That is not very reassuring."

"Indeed, it is not, but it is the truth."

"And Trefor is nothing if not honest," his aunt inserted.

Kitty poked her feet out a little further. "These are new slippers. I have only worn them to one other ball while in town."

Mr. Linton stood and held out his hand to her as the dancers, who were on the floor, began to exit it. "I shall do my best not to ruin them."

~*~*~

As it happened, Mr. Linton did an excellent job of keeping her slippers safe, for other than two stumbles where he seemed to forget his steps, he had danced very well. Kitty was certain, as she made her way to the retiring room with her sister, that she would not hesitate to accept him as a dance partner again.

"Miss Bennet!"

Kitty stopped on the staircase and turned to see Mr. Linton hurrying after her. "It looks as if he has my fan," she said to Elizabeth. "I will join you in a moment."

"Are you certain?"

"You have been waiting this age for me. Go. I will be well."

Her sister looked relieved and hurried on her way.

"My aunt thought you would not wish to lose this." Mr. Linton said as he bounded down the steps toward her. "And so, I told her I would return it to you." He came to a stop two steps below her.

"That was kind of you," she said as she accepted the fan from him. He looked as if he wanted to say something else. However, when he did not, she began to feel foolish and moved to step to the side and continue down the steps to the lower floor where the retiring room was located. However, making a neat and tidy exit was not to be, for in her haste, Kitty caught her toe on the hem of her dress, and then, Mr. Linton caught her.

"Are you well?" he asked as he held her in his embrace.

"Yes, yes, I am well." Mortified, but well. It was only her pride that hurt.

He brushed a curl away from her face. "Are you certain?"

She nodded, unable to speak while he looked at her so intently. Then, his head lowered towards her before he suddenly straightened and released her abruptly.

"If you are well," he muttered.

"Yes, thank you," she replied, feeling a trifle con-fused by his sudden cool manner.

"Then, I am glad I could be of service." He bowed and left her standing there, looking after him as he fled up the steps.

She raised a brow and shook her head. Mr. Lin-ton was so odd. She fingered the curl he had brushed aside as frustration welled inside of her. He really should have offered his arm and seen her safely down the last few steps, but instead, he fled! Feeling very much as if she had been abandoned,

Kitty hurried down the steps and to the retiring room to find her sister.

Chapter 9

"What has you skulking in the garden?"

Trefor looked up from examining the ground to find his friend Charles Edwards standing next to him. "I did not hear you approach."

"That is obvious. Now, what has you out here? Your sister is concerned which, in turn, means Evelyn is also worried." He leaned against the balustrade next to where Trefor was looking out into the small garden.

"I cannot do this." Trefor turned and motioned to the ballroom. "I think I might retire to the country early."

"You know you cannot do that. There are two weddings you must attend."

Trefor blew out a breath and shook his head. "I can return when needed. Aunt Gwladys can see to Connie and whatever needs doing there. Besides,

I should see that her things are made ready to be delivered to Crawford's. And if I stay in town, my aunt will expect me to escort her to every function so she can find me a wife."

"And that is a problem because... you do not wish to find a wife?"

Trefor scrubbed his face with his hands. "No. I will need one eventually."

"But you do not want one?" Charles pressed.

"No. I would very much like to marry – eventually – when I have found a lady who interests me in such a fashion. I do not want a pretty face with feathers for brains." He wanted someone to whom he could talk about anything and everything, but also someone who he would wish to take to bed for pleasure and not just to dutifully sire the required heir.

"Miss Bennet is interesting."

Charles was looking at him with that smug expression like he had at the literary reading and just as he had in the hallway at Mrs. Verity's. It was not a look Trefor felt needed a response.

"And she is pretty," Charles added.

Trefor grunted his reluctant agreement. Miss

Bennet was more than just pretty. She was intoxi-cating.

"And I doubt she has feathers for brains if she is happy at a literary reading," Charles said.

Again, Trefor grunted but added a shrug this time. She likely enjoyed poetry as much as novels and would be willing to read such to him. He would not find it a trial to listen to her for he imag-ined she would read with great expression just as she spoke with animation.

"She dances well."

"And what does that qualify her for?" Trefor grumbled.

"You would always have an excellent dance part-ner."

A delightful partner to be precise.

"I do not intend to dance once I am married," Trefor objected.

"You do plan to have children, do you not?"

"Of course."

"And they will need to be introduced to society, will they not?"

"As long as I have boys, I shall not need to escort them."

Charles chuckled. "You can no more guarantee

that than you can determine the yield of next year's wheat harvest."

A scowl settled over Trefor's face and mind. It was not that he never expected to dance again after he married. He quite liked a country dance now and again. However, he would not need to do it several times a month for several months of the year while his aunt whispered about this or that lady's qualifications.

He should just take a walk around the room, examine the ladies present, and pick the best of the lot so he could be done with it. Not unlike how he chose his horse – which had proven to be an excellent choice.

Again, he scrubbed his face. He could not make this a business transaction. A wife was not something you put out to pasture if she was not a good fit.

"I just cannot do this any longer," he muttered as he turned and looked out at the garden. "Do you know what I did tonight?" He glanced at Charles, who was still looking rather amused at his friend's plight. What Trefor was about to say would likely send the fellow into peals of laughter that would double him over with their intensity.

"No, I really could not guess." Charles turned to lean one hip on the balustrade so that he could look at Trefor.

A breeze rustled the branches below them.

"I nearly kissed her." Trefor braced himself for the hilarity to come, but to his surprise, Charles was absolutely silent.

"Miss Bennet," Trefor clarified.

Still, Charles said not a word for a full minute.

"At a ball?"

"Yes, yes, that is where we are," Trefor snapped. "We were on the steps leading down to the ground floor."

"Here? Tonight?"

It was as if his friend was slow of understanding. "Yes, when and where else would it have been? I have only known the vexing woman for two days."

That caused his friend's eyebrows to lift. "Vexing?"

There was no use in attempting to gingerly step around the subject, Edwards was not the sort to let a curious bit of news die until he had heard the whole story. He was frightfully inquisitive.

"I cannot put two words together without my tongue running ahead of my brain – not that the grey matter between my ears is even capable of rational thought when Miss Bennet is present." He shifted. "It is not as if I have not been in the presence of many pretty young debutantes. I have. And on each of those occasions, I have performed remarkably well – charmingly, even. But not with her.

"With her, I offend. I say things I did not know I had said, and I find myself nearly kissing a lady on the steps at a ball. And I cannot even apologize to her for my behavior since I will likely make it worse by saying something that I should not say or that she will not take as I meant it."

Charles chuckled. "You could start with will you marry me and extend this delicious torture forever."

"That will not do." The mere thought made his heart race and not in a pleasant fashion but more like he imagined it would when faced by an adder.

"I do not see why not," Charles retorted. "I would put money on it that even if you hie off to the country, she will follow you. However, I have sworn off bets, so you can keep your money."

Trefor only shook his head and turned his attention to the garden. Marriage had never before sent his heart flying like a skittish horse after hearing a loud clap of thunder. It had always been a topic which he could discuss in the calm, serious tone such an important matter deserved. He blamed Miss Bennet for that. She was the cause of his world being on end.

"I never thought to hear you say that you kissed a lady at a ball," Charles muttered.

"For good reason," Trefor replied. "And it was almost kissed. *Almost.* I did not kiss her." No matter how much he wished even now that he had.

Good heavens! What was wrong with him?

It was most probably due to the fact that he had spent far too much time with rapscallions like Edwards and Crawford. A bad apple was never improved by placing it with the good ones. He should have known that eventually, the company he kept would cause him some trouble.

His brow furrowed. Reprobate friends and decaying morals aside, he needed to apologize to Miss Bennet for taking such liberties as he had. But how?

"Are you returning to the dancing?" Charles asked.

Trefor shook his head. "I think it best if I do not."

"And how much of this conversation shall I share with Mrs. Kendrick when explaining why it is best if you do not?"

"You are the worst friend," Trefor grumbled.

"No, that would be Crawford. I am not marrying your sister."

Trefor shook his head. "Crawford is not out here threatening to tell my aunt about how Miss Bennet has my head in a muddle."

This was met with a chuckle.

"No, I believe he has arranged to meet your sister in an alcove and was unavailable for this task."

"He has done what?" Trefor growled.

"They are betrothed," Charles cautioned as Trefor moved to enter the building. "Which, of course, will mean that Henry is not *almost* kissing her."

"How long until the two of you wed your ladies so I can be rid of this town?"

"At the end of the season, which I believe was a suggestion that you made to Crawford and Mrs. Barrett decided was a good one for me as well."

"Well, it was a stupid one," Trefor grumbled.

"I would not argue that point."

Of course, his friend would not. The past several weeks were the longest single stretch of time that Edwards had ever comported himself appropriately with a lady. Trefor stopped just inside the ballroom. "You are changed."

"How so?" Charles eyed him warily.

"You do not seek out alcoves and flirt."

"True."

"Will it remain this way?"

Charles nodded his head.

"Because of a lady?" A sinking feeling filled Trefor's being.

"Yes. A very demanding, yet excessively wonderful, lady, whom I love more than alcoves, stolen kisses, and even life itself."

Had the room grown warmer while he was outside or was it just coming in from the coolness of the night that made Trefor wish to mop his brow?

"Are you well?" Edwards asked him.

Trefor nodded but then shook his head. "I hardly know."

His friend slapped him on the back. "Ah, but you will know, eventually. We all do."

Trefor followed behind his friend who was far

too optimistic at times such as right now when Trefor felt that his world was tilted in the wrong direction and would never be righted.

"I see you found him," Aunt Gwladys said when they joined her.

"He has a bit of a headache," Charles said.

"Do you need to go home?" his aunt asked.

Trefor considered it for a moment. He did not actually have a headache, but he was not feeling quite right. "It might be best." Not that retiring early would cure what ailed him.

"I will see if Mrs. Barrett will see Constance home," his aunt replied.

"You do not need to leave," Trefor protested. "I can take a hack."

"Are you certain?"

"Positive." He wanted to be alone. He needed to be alone. He did not need to have an aunt questioning him about his wellbeing, and he knew Aunt Gwladys would.

"Well, then, we will see you tomorrow."

He nodded. Of course, she would expect him to be in bed when she got home, and he would be. Whether or not he would be sleeping or merely staring at the ceiling feeling just as bewildered as he did now remained to be seen.

Quickly, he made his way out of the ballroom and down the stairs. He was just retrieving his hat from the butler when he was struck with a solution to his problem.

"Would you happen to have paper and a pen that I could use to leave a message for someone?"

"Of course, Mr. Linton. If you will follow me."

Just down the hall in a pleasant library, he was shown to a writing desk.

"I will be near the door if you need me to deliver it for you," the butler said before leaving him.

Trefor smoothed the paper and dipped his pen in the ink.

> *Miss Bennet,*
>
> *I should likely reserve this apology until next we meet when you call on my sister. However, I find that I am too unsettled to do as I should. You have a unique ability to unsettle me which is why I am writing this apology instead of speaking it. I am certain I would say something to offend but hope*

that in writing, I will be able to express myself in a better fashion.

My behaviour on the stairs tonight was not as it ought to have been. I should have released you as soon as I knew that you were no longer in danger of falling, but I could not. I do not know why I could not, but I could not. I promise you that I do not, as a practice, embrace young ladies or nearly kiss them as I did you. Again, I must repeat myself. You have a unique ability to unsettle me and cause me to do things I would not normally do.

Please forgive me for my behavior. I promise to respond in a more appropriate fashion whenever we next meet – even if you should once again fall into my arms.

I shall call on you tomorrow to learn my fate. Accept me if you will or send me away if you must.

Yours, etc.

Linton

He waited for the ink to dry, then folded the missive and left the library.

"Will you see that Mr. –" No, he could not give this to Mr. Darcy. There was no need for the gentleman to read it. "– Miss Bennet receives this? She is accompanied by Mr. and Mrs. Darcy this evening."

"I shall see that it is done straight away."

Feeling as if a small burden had been lifted, Trefor thanked the man and made his way out into the night to find his way home.

Chapter 10

"Good morning, Catherine." Mr. Gardiner looked up from his paper.

"Good morning, uncle," Kitty returned his greeting as she sat down at the table in the Gardiner's dining room to have a cup of tea. Was there a reason he used her full name?

Her uncle put his paper aside. His smile was pleasant. Perhaps he had just decided to use her full name for no particular reason.

"Your aunt informed me that you had an enjoyable evening."

"I did!" Kitty exclaimed. "I danced all but two sets."

It had been a delightful ball. She had never felt so wonderful as she had last evening with gentleman after gentleman asking her for a dance. It did not even bother her that some were likely doing it because they thought she had money. However, she had kept a list of names and would ask Mr. Linton when she saw him next. There were three days before she was promised to attend any soirees, so she had plenty of time to discover whatever she needed to know about each and every one of the gentlemen with whom she had danced.

"And I heard you lost your footing on the stairway."

Kitty blushed. "It was foolish. I caught my toe on my dress, but I did not fall."

"No, a gallant young man was there to catch you." He smiled at her. "Your aunt told me. She did not tell me if he has eyes that are bluer than Mr. Waller's, however."

Kitty laughed. "He does not. Mr. Waller's eyes are dark blue. Mr. Linton's are lighter and more silvery but very striking." In fact, they were the most captivating eyes she had seen last night. She quite liked them. Very much, truth be told.

"I also heard that he almost kissed you."

Kitty swallowed the sip of tea she had taken before turning startled eyes toward her uncle. She had not told her aunt that! In fact, she had not even been certain if Mr. Linton had intended to kiss her.

Her uncle was not looking at her but was spooning jam onto his toast.

"And," Uncle Gardiner continued as he spread the jam all the way to the edges of his bread, "I hear he is hoping for your acceptance of something – an offer of marriage was implied."

"You heard what?" Kitty forced the words out. Marriage? Acceptance? Of what was her uncle speaking?

"Just a bit of some fantastic tale in the paper. You know how it is, no names were given, but the clues are hard to miss."

"Paper?"

Her uncle sighed. "I had feared it was a fabricated concoction." He smiled softly at her. "I told your aunt we would have been told if any gentleman were to make an offer to you. I did not think you would keep anything so momentously happy from us."

"I do not know of what you speak." Panic, like an enormous wave, was swelling within Kitty and threatening to break over her and sweep her away when it withdrew from the shore.

Mr. Gardiner took a bite of his toast before picking up his paper. "Four lines," he said. "There is not much to it, just a little mention on the society page." He took another bite of his toast.

How could he eat when her life was hanging precariously close to a violent ocean eager to devour her? Kitty lifted her cup and with effort managed to swallow a bit of her tea.

"Here." He placed his finger on the page. "*Miss B, the new sister of Mr. F.D. of Derbyshire, has made quite the splash in her first season. It has been said Mr. T.L. of Suffolk is anxiously anticipating her reply to his letter of offer. Will there be happiness in store for Mr. T.L. or will he be left with only his memory of holding her in his arms and a near kiss and naught else?*"

A small amount of relief washed over Kitty. The mention of the kiss was disturbing, but the offer could be easily explained away, could it not? "It is only a rumour of an offer. That is not so bad, is it?"

Her uncle shrugged. "It really depends on how those who read it spin the tail. That bit about holding you in his arms and a near kiss is perhaps the worst of it."

That was what she had also feared. "But holding me in his arms could refer to a dance, could it not? There was no one on the stairs with me when I fell."

Again, her uncle shrugged. "It could very much refer only to a dance." His face grew serious. "Why would anyone expect an offer has been made by Mr. Linton? And what of the near kiss?"

Kitty shook her head. "I do not know. He did not kiss me. We talked during the first set, then danced the second, and then later met on the stairs. Could it be that he bent his head to hear me when we were dancing? Could that be a near kiss?" None had seen him bend his head towards her on the stairs.

Her uncle shrugged. "I could not say."

"He did not kiss me," Kitty reasserted. Not that she had not spent a portion of the night wondering if he had intended to and then considering whether or not she wished he had. "After saving me from falling on the stairs, he disappeared. His sister said he was on the terrace and then later Mr. Edwards said Mr. Linton had gone home with a headache."

"He only danced the one set with you? He danced with no one else?"

Kitty shook her head. "He danced once with his sister and another time with Miss Barrett – Mr. Edward's betrothed. Then, he left."

"Then, you were the only lady, other than those of his intimate circle, with whom he danced?"

"Yes."

"I am not well-versed in the gossip of the ton, but when I was courting your aunt, to attend an assembly and only dance with your sister and her friend and then one other lady was seen as paying special attention to that other lady. Such a thing always brought talk of betrothals."

"Oh, dear." Kitty slumped into her chair. "What does this mean for me?"

Her uncle blew out a breath. "I cannot say for certain. It really does depend upon how the gossips weave the tail. I will speak with Mr. Darcy and see what he says. You did not receive a letter from Mr. Linton, did you?"

Kitty shook her head. She knew that correspondence from a gentleman was not something of which Mama would approve if the gentleman had not received permission from her uncle or Mr. Darcy to send her letters. Much could be misconstrued from accepting such. Why, according to Mama, a lady who corresponded with a gentleman was as good as betrothed to the fellow.

"Oh," she groaned. "Must I marry him?"

Her uncle shook her head. "I do not think that things are so serious as that."

Oh, but if she had to! She took a deliberate sip of her tea. It tasted bland and not at all as welcoming as it should – much like her perfect ball had been turned into part of a terrible dream.

"He is not dreadful," she said. But he was disagreeable, and she knew so little about him. She had not thought to ask about his estate or what desserts he preferred or if he liked hunting and riding. She only knew that he liked to argue with her and did not always stop to think before he spoke.

She took another sip of her flavourless tea. It was at least warm. There was a little comfort in that, as there was also some comfort in knowing that she liked both Mrs. Kendrick and Miss Linton. If she were forced to marry Mr. Linton, she would at least have a sister and an aunt she admired.

Marry Mr. Linton? It was a thought with such finality. She had hoped to meet several gentlemen and be called on and taken for drives and such before two or three of them presented their offers. She would then deliberate and choose the one that grieved her heart the most to think of losing.

"I have only just begun my season," she whispered. "It cannot be over before it has begun."

Her uncle rose from his place, came around the table, and placed a hand on her shoulder. "We must not fret about things we do not know. Will you still be going to Elizabeth's for calling hours as planned?"

"Do you think I should?"

"Your aunt thought it best. We must know what is being said and how you will be received. However, you are staying with us, and it would be no big thing for Elizabeth to inform callers that you were unable to join her."

Stay here and wait to hear her fate rather than discover it as soon as possible? It was tempting to hide, but then one could not hide from worry and curiosity. "I will go."

And she did go. In fact, she and her aunt were half an hour early to their time, but neither Mr. Darcy nor Elizabeth seemed disturbed by that. In fact, it came as a relief to them, for they had wished to speak to Kitty about the article in the paper and one other thing.

"You were given what?" Kitty could not believe what her sister had just said.

"A letter from Mr. Linton to you. You were dancing at the time, and I put it in my reticule and promptly forgot until I was home. I did not think it was something which needed to be delivered to you before you arrived today."

"What does it say?" Kitty could not imagine what Mr. Linton had to write to her about.

"I did not read it."

"Nor did I," Darcy said. "Although I wished to."

Elizabeth laughed. "He was not pleased that the gentleman had left you a letter and had dispatched a footman to give it to you at a ball."

"Indeed," Darcy agreed flatly. "If a gentleman is going to give a letter to a lady, firstly, there should be a very good reason, and secondly, it should be done privately so that not all in attendance knows it has been done."

"Does everyone know that he left me a letter?" Oh! She should have allowed the horrid beast guarding the logs at the great tree to devour him!

"My husband exaggerates." Elizabeth's smile for Mr. Darcy was teasing. "You did not know about the letter, so therefore, it only stands to reason that not everyone in attendance knows about that letter. In fact, it was delivered in a somewhat discreet fashion. I am certain that not more than three of four ladies near me heard the footman say that Mr. Linton had left a message for Miss Bennet and would I be able to give it to her."

Kitty scowled. "He does the stupidest things!"

Mr. Darcy chuckled. "My guess is that he is not usually so stupid. He may have just gotten off on the wrong foot and has no idea how to regain his footing."

Kitty raised a brow. It was not just that Mr. Linton had made a bad first impression. He had made very few good impressions at all in the two days she had known him.

"This is the letter," Elizabeth took a paper from the table beside her. "Mr. Darcy would like to see it, of course, but the decision is yours."

"And you do not wish to see it?" Aunt Gardiner asked Elizabeth with a laugh.

"She was more curious about it last night than I was," Darcy replied.

"And it has been a trial not to peek at it," Elizabeth agreed.

"Oh, my!" Kitty exclaimed. He had almost kissed her! She had not been mistaken. It was somewhat delightful to inspire a handsome gentleman to wish to kiss her, even if it was entirely unexpected and improper.

"What is it?" Elizabeth asked.

Kitty blushed. "An apology." She glanced at her aunt. "You see I almost fell down the stairs last night after Mr. Linton returned my fan to me."

"You what?" Elizabeth exclaimed.

"Mr. Linton saved her," Aunt Gardiner said. "She told me about it before she went to bed."

"And you did not tell me?"

"She did not wish for you to feel badly about doing as she said and going on to the retiring room without her," Aunt Gardiner said.

"And if this letter had not caused the issues it has..." Kitty pressed her lips together. Her excuses were not lessening the look of displeasure on her sister's face. "I truly did not wish to worry you." She took one more look at her letter and then handed it to her sister. "You may read it."

She knew she had to let them read it, but that did not make her heart hammer any less as Elizabeth read the missive.

"Oh, my, indeed," Elizabeth said before handing the letter to Mr. Darcy.

Everyone waited silently as each person was

given a chance to read the letter. Or more precisely, they waited silently except for the small exclamation each made in turn as they read it. Apparently, Mr. Linton wishing to kiss Kitty was just as shocking to them as it was to her.

Aunt Gardiner was just folding the letter and saying, "Well, it seems our Kitty has an admirer," when the butler entered the room and announced...

"Mr. Linton to see Miss Bennet and Mr. Darcy."

Chapter 11

Trefor shifted from foot to foot as he stood, waiting to be allowed entrance to the Darcy's sitting room.

This morning, he had practised his confession to his aunt, his sister, and Crawford. Edwards had not been home when he called, or Trefor would have given his speech to Charles as well.

However, now that he stood here, knowing that *she* was in the sitting room, no amount of practice could keep his thoughts in a tidy order in his head.

She was frustratingly distracting. He closed his eyes but just as had happened when he had attempted to sleep last night, enchanting hazel eyes, beautiful brown hair, and animated features were all he could see.

"Mr. Linton," the butler's voice broke through Trefor's thoughts, "they will see you now."

"Right. Good. Thank you." He looked at the hat in his hand and then held it out to the butler. "Keep it close. I may be sent packing rather quickly." Hopefully, in one piece.

The man nodded and took the hat.

With a final deep breath, he willed his mind to order itself and walked into the sitting room.

"Good day," he bowed to Mr. Darcy and his wife before giving a bow of his head to the lady sitting next to Miss Bennet. Then...

Then, he looked at *her*. And all hope was indeed lost. Not a rational thought remained in his head. So, he plunged forward hoping that he would not overly offend anyone, but most especially Miss Bennet.

"It seems that in my attempt to correct my poor behaviour I have made a muck of things and find myself yet again – or still – in need of apologizing."

"Please, be seated," Mr. Darcy offered.

"Are you sure you wish that?" Trefor asked. "Miss Bennet's name appeared in the paper because of me."

"Yes, I know. Now, sit."

"Of course, sir." Trefor did as he was instructed. He did not need to anger anyone further than they might already be angered. He blew out a breath and rubbed his hands on the top of his thighs. This room was excessively warm.

"Are you well?" Miss Bennet asked him.

He shook his head. "No, and I have not been since you crashed into me two days ago."

"Me? Crash into you? I believe it was you who did the crashing."

This was not a good start to things. Not at all. "You are correct."

"I am?" She blinked at him in surprise.

"Yes. Unless you would like me to say you are not." His eyes were fixed on Miss Bennet, but to his right, he could hear Mr. Darcy chuckle. That was odd. A gentleman whose relation had been named in a story in the paper should not be chuckling – not that Trefor was about to point that out to the gentleman.

Miss Bennet's brow furrowed. "Do you think I am correct or not?"

"I have very little clue as to what I think," he answered honestly. "But considering how we first met and knowing that I was exiting the drawing room in haste and a foul mood, it is most likely that you are indeed correct." He glanced from her to the lady beside her. He had seen her before. Of course, he could not, at his moment, place where.

"This is my aunt, Mrs. Gardiner. Aunt, this is Mr. Linton."

Ah! That was it.

"We are not complete strangers," Mrs. Gardiner said.

"No, indeed, we have seen each other in passing at Mrs. Verity's," Trefor agreed. "However, I have never officially met you, and if it were not for the present circumstances, I would say it is a pleasure to finally meet. Not that meeting you now is unpleasant – it is the circumstances that are unpleasant." He cast a worried look at Kitty as he once again heard Mr. Darcy chuckle. Perhaps his discomfort and apparent ineptitude was satisfaction enough for Mr. Darcy.

"I did not think that my leaving you a message would end with your name in the paper, Miss Bennet." He slipped a finger behind his cravat and pulled at it to try to loosen it some. The room was only growing warmer.

"However, as my sister and my aunt and even Crawford have reminded me, it was poor form to write to a lady without permission from her guardian and some sort of understanding, which two days ago, I would have known."

"It is rather shocking," Miss Bennet said. "I only received it and read it this morning."

His brow furrowed and he looked from Miss Bennet to Mrs. Darcy and then her husband. "I do not understand. The butler said that he would see it was given to Miss Bennet straight away."

"My sister was dancing, and so it was given to me," Mrs. Darcy replied. "I only remembered it once we were home last night and so did not give it to Kitty until just before you arrived."

"Truly?" He had been certain that someone had been reading over Miss Bennet's shoulder or some such thing and that was how the content of his letter had become known. "Then, how?"

"Did you think I told the paper?"

His head snapped toward Miss Bennet. "No, I thought the letter had been seen by someone when you were reading it or dropped and read before it was returned to you."

"The gentry are not the only ones who can read and gossip," Mrs. Gardiner said.

Of course! Trefor ran a hand through his hair.

"Apparently, I overlooked that fact as well when I launched my brilliant plan."

"Such things can happen," Mr. Darcy agreed.

Trefor's brow furrowed. The man was too agreeable. But then, nothing had been as it was supposed to be since meeting Miss Bennet. Therefore, he really should not be so startled by Mr. Darcy's lack of stamping and snorting.

"I do not understand how such things can happen," Miss Bennet said.

"You are unsettling," Trefor replied. "As I said in my letter. I did say that, did I not?"

"Yes, you did," Mr. Darcy replied.

He had read the letter and still was not fuming? Trefor thought he had mentioned nearly kissing Miss Bennet in there somewhere. He was almost positive of it.

"I also do not see how I can be unsettling," Kitty said.

"But you are," Trefor assured her. "I assure you that I am a very proper sort of fellow – normally – before you crashed into me." Her eyebrows rose. "Forgive me. Before you crashed into me. No, no, that is not it. Before I crashed into you. I simply cannot think straight around you."

"That is ridiculous," Miss Bennet scoffed.

"I agree," Trefor assured her, "but it is also true." He blew out a breath. "Where do we go from here?" He turned his eyes back toward Mr. Darcy.

"I would suggest a courtship," Mr. Darcy replied.

"A what?" Miss Bennet exclaimed.

"A courtship," Darcy repeated. "There are those who have read the paper who will expect that Mr. Linton has made some sort of offer for you. Any sort of gossip that might ensue can be more easily turned aside if we present an amicable friendship to one and all, and the wags will find something more interesting to discuss."

"But a courtship?" Miss Bennet pressed. "A courtship precedes a betrothal."

"It can," Mr. Darcy agreed, "but only if the young lady accepts an offer of marriage once one is made. For now, you are only agreeing to discover who Mr. Linton is and if you will suit."

"A courtship?" Miss Bennet repeated.

"Yes," Mr. Darcy answered, "I propose that Mr. Linton call on you regularly as would be expected by those who might be watching. He will dance with you at balls – two sets. He can take you for drives and whatever else he might think to do as a suitor, and then you can decide after a period of time if things should continue or be dissolved. Are you agreeable to that, Mr. Linton?"

"If Miss Bennet is," Trefor replied. "It seems a sensible plan."

"But no other gentlemen will call on me," Miss Bennet protested.

"And Mr. Linton will give up calling on any other ladies," Mr. Darcy countered.

"I have never been to town before." Miss Bennet's voice was soft enough to prick Trefor's heart.

"Other gentlemen can still dance with you at balls," he offered, "and if one of them catches your interest –" Oh! That hurt. "—you have only to say so, and I will step away."

"Are you certain this is the best way?" Miss Bennet asked Mr. Darcy.

"I would agree that it is," Mrs. Gardiner said.

"As would I," Elizabeth added. "Mr. Linton is very generous to be willing to give up so much and then step aside as a gentleman who has been shunned if you decide on another." She glanced at him. "And I think he understands what is being asked of you."

"Indeed, I am grieved that you must be put in

this situation," he said. "I assure you that this was not my intent whatsoever."

A pretty, though sad, pout formed on her lips. "You are not dreadful," she said.

"I am flattered," he replied flatly, earning him a small smile.

"At least not when you are not being disagreeable. Do you suppose you could refrain from arguing with me?"

"I do not argue with you. You argue with me."

Her eyebrows rose.

"I shall make an attempt, but I cannot promise," he adjusted. "You are provoking."

"Really, Mr. Linton. I am both unsettling and provoking?"

Her eyes were sparkling. He was not doomed to being the fellow who had stolen the light from her eyes. That was a relief.

"Yes, quite."

"I do not see what about me is either unsettling or provoking."

"Have you no mirror?" The thought was out of his mouth before he could capture it.

"Of course, I have a mirror. I do not see what that has to do with anything."

He cast a nervous glance in Mr. Darcy's direction. The gentleman was looking excessively amused. Yes, the man must be taking great satisfaction in Trefor's unease. With that in mind, Trefor hurled himself into what was likely going to be a humiliating admission to make in front of a lady who only deemed him "not horrid."

"Have you used it?"

"My mirror?" Miss Bennet's brows were lifted high.

"Yes."

"Why would I have a mirror and not use it?"

Trefor shrugged. "I would think that one would use a mirror if she had one, and if you have, then you must be aware of one reason why you are profoundly unsettling."

Her brow furrowed.

"You are beautiful."

"Oh!" Her cheeks grew rosy, and her lips turned up into a pleased smile.

"And what makes her provoking?" Mr. Darcy's voice was laced with amusement.

"Her infernal compulsion to argue with me." Trefor smiled sheepishly. "And, more often than not, be correct."

"Yes," Darcy said with a chuckle, "I believe that runs in the family."

"Being correct does," Mrs. Darcy inserted.

Mrs. Gardiner simply laughed, letting Trefor know that what was said must be true.

"I am correct?" Miss Bennet asked.

"Many times," he answered.

A smile spread across her face. "Thank you. I do not think I have been told that before." She tipped her head. "You are really quite charming when you are agreeable. Yes, I think we shall affect a courtship."

"Are you certain you can tolerate it?" Trefor teased.

"No, but we must try." She batted her lashes as she spoke.

Real or no, Trefor expected he was going to enjoy courting Miss Bennet.

"Then, shall we start with a drive in the park?"

"Today?"

Trefor nodded. "If that is acceptable with Mr. Darcy and your aunt."

"But I do not have my driving bonnet."

He could tell from the worried look on her face that she was not just putting forward an excuse to put him off. "Then, tomorrow. If your aunt would be so kind as to tell me where I can collect you."

"Only," Mrs. Gardiner said, "if you agree to come to dinner when you are through. Lizzy and Mr. Darcy, as well as my children, will be there."

"I would be delighted." Trefor rose. "This ended more agreeably than I expected." He gave a bow of his head to Mr. Darcy. "I thank you for not blackening my eye as I did to the gentleman whose name was linked in the paper to my sister's."

Darcy chuckled. "If your reputation had been what Mr. Edwards' was, I likely would have."

"I thank you just the same." He turned to Miss Bennet. "And thank you for agreeing to allow me to pretend to court you." He paused before turning to leave. "Am I forgiven for my improper behavior and not thinking through my solution of sending you a letter?"

Her lips pursed, but her eyes were dancing. "Oh, your quest has just begun, Mr. Linton. However, telling me I was both beautiful and correct was a fine start."

"And how long shall my quest be?" He must remember that she was a romantic and, as most romantics were, was likely given to flights of fancy.

"I believe the standard is three tests, which means you have to successfully complete two more." She held up a finger. "But you cannot just repeat what you have done today, nor can I tell you what you must do for part of the trial is the discovery. Otherwise, a transformation is not real. It must come from your soul."

"Well, then, I look forward to continuing the quest tomorrow." He tipped his head. "Would flowers help?"

She laughed lightly. "I cannot tell you, Mr. Linton."

"That is a pity. I have already proven myself rather inept where you are concerned. It could be a lengthy quest."

"Or, you might never complete it." She batted her lashes as she spoke.

"Provoking. Utterly provoking," he muttered before taking his leave.

Chapter 12

Kitty pressed the top of her pen against her lip as she thought.

"You look perplexed," her aunt said.

"I am." She sighed. "Mr. L in my story..." She glanced sheepishly at her aunt. "He is who the story is about."

"Yes, I know."

Kitty's face pulled into a slight grimace. "He is also Mr. Linton." She tried not to feel the sting of guilt that accompanied the confession, but it could not be avoided.

"Does your uncle know this?" Her aunt was making a valiant effort not to smile as she applied herself to her knitting.

Uncle Gardiner had read the beginning of Kitty's story just yesterday. He had been impressed with the cause of the worn jacket and the curse that had been cast on poor Mr. L. It had been quite encouraging to hear his thoughts on her work. He had not teased, nor had he looked as if he was attempting to be kind.

"I do not think he does." At least, she had not told him; however, her uncle was very clever, so it was possible that he had figured it out.

"Are you worried that you have treated Mr. L far more harshly than he deserves by cursing him as you have?"

Kitty's brow furrowed. "Do you know the story?"

"I am afraid your uncle told me last night. He is quite taken with it."

That was a pleasant thought. Having someone as keen as her uncle enjoying the story not only enough to tell her how much he liked it, but also to share it with her aunt was something of importance and should be given its due consideration and the honour it deserved. So, Kitty allowed the feeling to settle into her chest before she continued to speak.

"It is not that Mr. L does not deserve his punishment. He was very rude, but..." She tapped her lip with her pen again. "Mr. Linton did say I was beautiful and right yesterday."

She glanced at her aunt whose hands were still, her knitting momentarily forgotten, as she waited for Kitty to continue. "It is just that perhaps I did not consider why Mr. L was rude in my story."

She placed her pen on the little groove of the writing desk she was using. "What if he was cursed by accident? What if he is not truly as horrid as I first thought? I must consider these things now that we are to be friends."

She still could not bring herself to admit that they were courting. Friends was a step far enough. She was not prepared to think beyond that.

"What did you have planned to happen to Mr. L in your story?" Her aunt asked. "Were you going to feed him to a dragon or have him drawn and quartered?"

Kitty shook her head. "I had considered allowing the beast at the great tree to eat him, but then, my story would be over before it began, and the boy's mother would never regain her health."

"And at the end? Would Mr. L still have all his limbs?"

Kitty shrugged. "Most likely."

"I am afraid, then, that I do not see the dilemma."

"You do not?" How could her aunt not see it? How was she supposed to torment a friend – even if it was only imaginarily done? Kitty was certain that Mary would say that it was not right to do so.

"Your Mr. L has a quest to complete, does he not?"

"Yes."

"And can he not face the obstacles set before him and rise heroically above them?"

"I suppose he could."

"Would it not be possible for him to discover how he became to be as rude as he was and then learn to not be so again? Discovering such a thing would be a delightful treat for your uncle to read."

"Do you really think so?"

Her aunt nodded. "He does like an interesting turn of events now and again." She smiled at Kitty. "He is very imaginative himself."

"I had no idea."

"I am certain very few do since he applies his imagination to his work. Only I get to hear the occasional tale he tells one or another of the children." She picked up her knitting. "I think your dilemma lies in your motivation."

Kitty's brow furrowed.

"Why did you decide to write your story about Mr. L?"

"Oh!" Kitty gasped as understanding dawned. She had been angry with Mr. Linton.

"You may either punish your character, or you can help him improve." Her aunt looked up from her knitting. "The two are not the same."

Kitty had set about writing to have a way to make Mr. L suffer. Her cheeks grew warm. Mary would most certainly not approve of someone being vengeful, even in a story.

"Helping someone improve is a very good thing," her aunt added. "A loving thing even."

"I do not love Mr. Linton."

Her aunt chuckled. "I did not mean to say you did. One can be loving without falling in love with someone."

"That is true," Kitty muttered. She was almost sure it was true. It was most certainly true of sisters and cousins, as well as her friends who were not handsome with silvery blue eyes.

"Who knows, you might just find you can love Mr. Linton."

"No," Kitty said emphatically with a firm shake of her head for emphasis.

"He is not a poor option to consider. Your mother would approve of him, do you not think?"

Would she? Kitty's head tipped. She had not stopped to consider what Mama would think of Mr. Linton other than to conclude after their first meeting that Mama would not like him. Mama did not like anyone who did not treat her daughters as she thought they deserved to be treated. Why just look at how she had not liked Mr. Darcy after the assembly! And he had not mistaken Elizabeth for a servant! He had only said she was not tempting. Not being handsome enough to tempt a gentleman was no small thing but to be thought a maid and so far beneath his notice was something far worse. Kitty was certain of it.

However, if her aunt thought that Mama would approve, there must be a reason. Kitty searched for things that would recommend Mr. Linton to her mother.

"He has an estate, though I do not know how large." Mama had always insisted that her daughters should marry someone who owned land and the more, the better.

"And a house in town," her aunt added. "A gentleman with a house in town and an estate is most likely not poor. Mr. Linton does not seem the sort of man to squander his fortune. He was prompt to apologize for his error. That could not have been easily done. Arriving at a gentleman's house to admit that he had placed a sister's reputation in question had to have been a fearful thing."

It had indeed appeared that Mr. Linton was fearful yesterday when he arrived at Darcy House. And so, it seemed he was honourable underneath all his stumbling and bumbling. Not that Kitty wished to admit it to her aunt just yet. It seemed far too soon to be so approving.

"He is handsome." That she could admit. His features were easily admired by one and all. A lady did not need to know a gentleman at all to comment on his appearance.

"I will not argue that. And he is quite tall and broad."

Yes, Mr. Linton was a fine example of what a desirable gentleman should be when observed from a distance. Which is from where Kitty would like to observe him – from a nice, safe distance. Once a lady drew closer to observe the object of her admiration, that was when things began to feel more intimate. That was when hopes and dreams could be aroused and dashed.

It was not that Kitty did not enjoy drawing closer to handsome men. A casual flirtation was an enjoyable thing and was an excellent way to discover if one wished to deepen the acquaintance. That was what Mama had always said. Of course, she had also said that, while engaging in a flirtation, a lady must be careful to keep her heart from being affected by every handsome face.

However, a courtship, even one which was only affected, was not a casual flirtation. It was something far more weighty, and so her mother's advice was not so very helpful.

Kitty was not even certain that Mr. Linton was capable of flirting. He was excellent at arguing and being disagreeable, but flirting and teasing? He would need to be able to think before blurting to accomplish that, and so far, in their acquaintance, he had not been able to carry off that particular skill — at least, not for more than a few sentences. Even in telling her she was beautiful, he had blurted. Telling someone to use a mirror to discover why they were unsettling was not precisely charming, although, she had to admit she had still enjoyed hearing that she was beautiful.

"You should change your dress and wash the ink off your fingers," her aunt said when Kitty once again picked up her pen. "Mr. L will be here soon." She winked at Kitty.

"Aunt!"

"I promise not to tease you too much, but I must say that I am excited for you."

"Why? He is only courting me because he must."

Her aunt shook her head. "No, you are only allowing him to court you because he must. I think he is quite willing to court you without any persuasion."

"We argue." Kitty placed her ink and pen in the small compartment for them in the desk and tucked her notebook inside the larger section, snapping it closed and turning her key in the lock.

"And so did Lizzy and Mr. Darcy."

"Aunt!" Kitty cried again.

"I am only hoping you will give him proper consideration."

Kitty stood with her writing desk in hand. "I

suppose it would be foolish not to consider him as one would a new friend, would it not?"

"Excessively."

Kitty blew out a breath as she mounted the stairs to her room to prepare to spend time with her new friend. Her new, handsome friend. Friend. She repeated the word to herself. That is what they were and naught else. Friends did not endanger one's heart, for one did not marry a friend, did she?

Such troubling thoughts were still perplexing Kitty when the source of her trouble walked into the sitting room looking very dashing in his black jacket and grey waistcoat.

"I know you could not tell me, but I thought it might be best to bring flowers anyway." Mr. Linton handed her a bundle of six daffodils.

"They are very cheerful," Kitty answered as she took them.

"I will make certain they are placed in your room," her aunt said. "There is nothing so nice as waking to fresh flowers." She took the daffodils from Kitty before adding, "And in your chamber, they will be safe from your cousins. I have had more than one bouquet picked clean of its buds.

Maxwell loves to present me with treasures even if those treasures are not new to me."

"Max is three," Kitty said to fill the void when her aunt left the room.

"I am afraid I do not know much about children," Mr. Linton said.

"Then, I suppose you do not know if you like them or not."

"I suppose I do not, but I imagine I would like them." His face scrunched. "Or I hope I will. It is expected of a gentleman to have children so that there is an heir to the estate and all that."

Kitty nodded as she was not certain how else to reply to such a statement.

"And do you like children, Miss Bennet?"

"Yes, very much."

"You will wish to have a large family, I assume."

Friends. She repeated to herself once again. Friends could speak of wishes for families and the like. She had spoken to both Lydia and Maria Lucas about such things. However, neither her sister nor their particular friend made Kitty's stomach flutter as Mr. Linton did, and that, along with the thought of being the mother of his children, which would not be pushed out of her mind, made this conversation much different than any she had ever had before about the topic, for while it was a conversation that two friends might have, it felt far more personal to discuss such a thing with him.

"I would not be opposed to such a thing. I have four sisters, after all."

"Right, right." He tugged at his waistcoat.

"And do you wish for a large family?" Kitty could feel her cheeks growing warm at the question as if it were too impertinent to ask. However, it had seemed only proper to inquire after his opinion until the words had exited her mouth.

"Two is expected, I believe. So, I would wish for at least two. I honestly have not considered it beyond that."

"You have not? Never?" Who did not think of the sort of family he wished to have? She had been thinking about it since she was twelve and understood that, one day, she would be a mother. Did boys just not think of such things or was it just Mr. Linton who did not?

"No, never. Is that wrong?" He looked pained.

"It is not wrong," Kitty assured him, though she secretly suspected it was. "It is just odd. I thought everyone thought about such things. The end result of marriage is to have a family, after all, and if one is seeking a husband or wife, I should think that such thoughts would be natural." Either her face was surely going to burst into flames, or her cheeks were going to melt off. Again, such commentary should have been confined to her mind. But he had surprised her. He was often surprising her and causing her to speak before she could think better of it.

"Perhaps it should be natural," he said in a strained voice.

Good, he was as uncomfortable as she. That did make her feel somewhat better.

"Do you have a maid to accompany you?" he asked. "If we are to reach the park and return in time for dinner, we should be off."

"Oh, yes, Fiona." She turned to the maid in the corner. "Are you ready to go?"

"Yes, ma'am," Fiona replied. "Do you require anything?"

"No, I have all I need."

"Then, if there are no other instructions of which I need to be aware, shall we leave?" Mr. Linton asked.

"I had hoped my aunt would return before we left."

"I can tell Mrs. Tuttle that we are going," Fiona offered.

"Thank you. That will work just as well." Relief washed over Kitty. "I did not wish to leave without my aunt knowing," she said to Mr. Linton.

"Shall we wait to see if she has any instructions?"

"No, I have been told the time we must be back for dinner and other than that, I am to enjoy myself but not so far as to kiss anyone." Oh, goodness! She really must learn to filter her words. "I should not have said that last bit. My uncle was teasing me this morning, you see. The story in the paper and all."

Mr. Linton offered her his arm to escort her to his waiting carriage. "My aunt was not teasing when she said the same thing to me."

A giggle burst out of Kitty without warning.

Mr. Linton chuckled. "It may come as no surprise to you, but I am not proficient at courting a lady. I have taken a lady or two for a drive. I am not unfamiliar with sitting in drawing rooms or dancing or escorting someone to the theater and the like, but I have never courted someone in a formal sense." He helped Kitty into his barouche.

"I have never been courted."

"Have you been to the theatre?" He climbed up and took his place beside her.

"Not yet."

His lips tipped into a smile. "Then, we shall have to correct such an oversight. You strike me as someone who would enjoy a play."

"Oh, I think I would." Very much. Especially if he was sitting as close to her as he was now. He smelled of fresh air and cedar. It was an intoxicating mix.

She tucked her skirts around her legs, carefully taking note that nothing of her person was closer than one hand's span away from Mr. Linton. For if it was, thinking of him as a friend and naught else was going to be excessively difficult. As it was, their private conversation and the closeness of his handsome person had her wishing to think of him as more.

Chapter 13

"Are you certain you wish to come inside with me?" Constance asked her brother as their carriage came to a stop in front of Mrs. Verity's.

"There must be something I could do in there that involves children." Miss Bennet liked children and had found it rather amusing that he had not known what to do with her youngest cousin, Lottie, when the child had climbed onto his lap in the Gardiner's sitting room after their meal two days ago.

"It is a home for children."

He glowered at his sister's amusement at his expense. "I know. That is why I assume there must be something I can learn about them here." He climbed out of the carriage and offered her his hand. "Miss Bennet thinks that one should both know if one likes children and if one wishes for a large family or a small one before he begins a season." He shrugged as he tucked Connie's hand into the crook of his arm.

"That does seem wise."

"It does now that I have thought about it."

"You never considered the size of family for which you wished?"

In his sister's tone, he heard the same utter disbelief he had heard in Miss Bennets' voice when she had asked nearly the same thing two days ago. Again, he felt as if he had missed some important lesson in school. "I have not. I know that two is standard, and the Lord may bless beyond that, of course. I just did not know that one was to set plans for such a thing. If I had known, I would have."

Constance laughed. "I am positive you would have. You are a very good planner. Your estate does very well under your watch."

It did. His income was as secure as it could be with only that which could be spared being invested in ventures which were not so proven as he would like. However, ventures must be made into the new and modern if an estate wished to not only survive to be passed on to a future generation but also if it was to prosper and even expand. And now that he had to consider laying aside funds for more than two children, he needed those ventures to thrive more than ever.

"Mother and Father only had us," he said by way of justifying his lack of planning beyond two children.

"It was not for lack of trying to have more," his sister countered.

Trefor blinked. "I beg your pardon." Had his parents wished for more than two children?

"I know you do not like it when I speak so plainly, but Mother told me that she lost two babies before you were born and one after. They were fortunate to have us." She pulled him back from knocking on the door. "They loved each other very much, and when a couple loves one another as Mother and Father did," her cheeks were rosy, and he cringed to hear her say what he knew she was going to say, "they do not limit themselves to only producing two children." Her eyes held his. "Do not make me say it any more plainly. Please use your excessive intelligence to decipher my meaning, or if you cannot, ask Mr. Edwards. I am certain he can present it to you in a more direct and much less proper fashion."

Trefor shook his head in disbelief and self-admonishment. His little sister had just begun a lesson on the duties and pleasures of marriage with him! "Please, do not say any more. I understand your meaning perfectly."

He lifted his hand to knock on the door but then dropped it. "What is wrong with me?" Things were so far from right in his mind.

"Could you clarify your meaning?" Her eyes sparkled with impertinence.

"I should have been able to decipher what you told me. I should have known that a gentleman who loves his wife will... Well, you know. Or I assume you do since you were just talking about it." He blew out a breath. "It is as if half of my brain has been stolen from me, and I would greatly like to get it back. I am not normally so stupid."

"Not normally, but on occasion."

He rolled his eyes at her teasing.

"You do tend to think in absolutes, and sometimes those absolutes do not bend enough for reality," she said softly.

"I like absolutes," he muttered. They were safe and unchanging.

"Love is not an absolute," his sister added.

"Love?" He lifted the knocker and let it fall.

"Yes, my dear brother. Love. I could no more put what love is supposed to be in a list of qualifications than you can slot it neatly into a column in your account book." She squeezed his arm. "Love is unpredictable. Take Henry, for instance. I did not expect the gentleman whom I would love would be anything like him. I imagined someone more like you or father. Proper, always in control of himself, forever knowing what was happening and why. However," she said as the door was opened, "Henry has what I need, and I have what he needs. We compliment each other. We are alike in some ways and so very different in others."

From the entryway, he nodded in greeting to Mrs. Verity, who was just entering the drawing room.

"Perhaps," his sister whispered when she retook his arm after having removed her outerwear, "the sort of lady you need is not a prim and proper debutante but rather a spirited, young lady who challenges you to think beyond your neat little picture of how things are."

He did not respond to her suggestion. He could not. At least, he could not do so coherently. He had been pondering such a young lady ever since his foolishness had placed him in a position that required him to court that very young lady.

"I have brought you another volunteer," Connie said as they entered the drawing room where Mrs. Verity was sitting quietly at the window doing absolutely nothing.

"That is good news." She motioned to the settee across from her. "And what skills do you possess, Mr. Linton?"

"He is good at reconciling accounts," Connie offered.

He was. Indeed, unlike most, he enjoyed adding rows of numbers and figuring percents and the like. However, that was not why he was here.

"Actually," he began, "I am less of a volunteer than a pupil."

His heart thumped uncomfortably loudly in his chest as if it were attempting to escape and dash away from the embarrassment that admitting his need of instruction was sure to bring.

Mrs. Verity's eyebrows rose. "How so?" Her head tipped as she studied him intently.

"It has been brought to my attention that I am lacking in knowledge of children." There. He had said it. Aloud. To someone other than his sister. And it was as discomfiting as he had imagined it would be.

Mrs. Verity chuckled. "Indeed?"

Trefor nodded. "I would very much like to learn what to do with them."

"What to do with them?"

Oh, she was enjoying his uneasiness far too much, and he wished to tell her so. However, he also needed her assistance.

"Yes, things such as about what does one speak to children, and what do they like to do?"

Mrs. Verity's lips pursed as she lowered her dancing eyes to study her hands for a moment before looking up at Trefor with a more composed expression on her face, though her eyes still carried her amusement. "What did you like to do when you were young, Mr. Linton? Did you have a favourite toy? Did you favour a particular book or game? What lessons did you love or loathe?"

That seemed simple enough. Incredibly simple

actually. So simple that he should have been able to think of it on his own, but he had not been. "I quite enjoyed doing sums," he answered, "I loved any book my mother read me, I had some blocks that the carpenter who was building a new partition in the stable made for me which I treasured, and riding. I loved to ride. I still do."

"Well, we have no horses, so riding with our children is out of the realm of possibilities. However, we do have some blocks and several books." She leaned forward. "You will find that our little ones, in particular, are very fond of being read to because they have not yet learned to decipher the words for themselves."

"You teach them to read?"

"We do." She stood. "Come along, Mr. Linton. Let's see if we can get you accustomed to our youngest residents."

"How young?" He was feeling rather anxious as he rose to follow Mrs. Verity.

"We are going to the nursery."

"The nursery?" He had hoped to start with somewhat older children before having to face the littlest ones. The older children could likely carry on a conversation about simple subjects, but Miss

Bennet's cousin had known very few words, and even then, those words had sounded more like babble than actual words to him.

"Yes, the nursery, Mr. Linton. Those children are far too young to participate in lessons, but, do not fear, there are blocks." She chuckled.

Why was it that everyone found such glee in his discomfort? He found no pleasure in it at all, and as they ascended the stairs, his discomfort rose with each step.

"It is just here," Mrs. Verity opened the door to a room which was busy with sound.

Trefor peeked inside. There were two infants lying in cradles while four others, who possessed various degrees of mobility, were playing on a rug and at a small table. "I might be too large for this room," he whispered to Mrs. Verity.

"You will fit. It is not a tiny room," she assured him.

No, the room was not tiny, but the occupants were.

"Martha." Mrs. Verity stepped inside the room ahead of Trefor. "This is Mr. Linton, and he would like for you to take a rest while he plays with the children."

Martha's eyes grew wide.

Mrs. Verity whispered something to the woman, and her features softened into a smile.

"I think if he is successful here, in a week or two, we might see how he does reading to the older children or perhaps he can help Frank learn his sums."

"That is an excellent plan," Martha agreed.

Trefor was not certain if he agreed or not as he looked down at a little person who had attached herself to his boot.

"Remember, Mr. Linton," Mrs. Verity said before she left him with Martha. "None of these children have parents."

Trefor swallowed and nodded. "Neither do I. Not any longer."

"See, you have something in common already," Mrs. Verity replied with a smile.

"Who is this little one?" he asked, looking down at a pair of dark, curious eyes which were peering up at him.

"That is Emily. She has just had her first birthday last week," Martha replied. "She seems fond of you."

"She does," he muttered.

"You may play with her. She is very good at play-ing," Martha encouraged.

"How do I do that?"

Martha chuckled. "Emily, where is your baby?"

"Baby?"

Martha gave him a sad smile as if he were the most unfortunate fellow. "Her doll."

"Oh, right. I did not have dolls. My sister did, but she never let me play with them." He crouched down to be closer to Emily's height. "Where is your baby?" He repeated what the nursemaid had said.

Emily smiled and toddled away to pick up a small doll made of cloth.

"Why did your sister not let you play with her dolls, Mr. Linton," Martha asked.

"I would hide them or send them on dangerous missions to capture foreign lands."

Martha laughed. "Then, I can understand why she would keep her dolls from you."

Trefor smiled at the woman. "I promise not to hide Emily's doll."

"And no dangerous missions?"

"Not a one."

"Baby." Emily shoved her doll at him, and he took it. "Book."

Trefor glanced at Martha. He was unfamiliar with the language infants spoke.

"She wants you to read to the baby."

"To a doll?"

"That is her baby," Martha said with a pointed look. "There is a chair over there in the corner that she favours for stories."

"Book," Emily said once again.

Trefor held his hand out toward her outstretched one, and she wrapped her hand around one of his fingers. "Where are the books?" he asked her.

She babbled something in reply as she led him to the corner. There was a book already lying on the chair. He gave her a boost as she climbed into the oversized rocking chair, which looked as if it was designed specifically for reading to a child, and snuggled into the corner leaving ample room for him. Both arms reached toward him. "Baby."

"Here you are."

As Trefor placed the doll in Emily's arms, the door opened, and he heard whispering. However, he dared not remove his eyes from Emily, who was holding the doll in one arm and attempting to pick up the book with her free hand.

"Allow me," he offered. Picking up the book, he settled into the chair. Only then did he see that the new arrival to the room was watching him very carefully with inquisitive hazel eyes. "Miss Bennet," he greeted with a nod of his head.

"Book!" Emily demanded.

"Yes, yes. Do forgive me. I promise I had not forgotten." He opened the book to the first story.

"*The story of the Two Cocks[1].*" He glanced at Emily, who was arranging her baby in her lap. "*There once was a Hen who lived in a farm-yard, and she had a large brood of chickens. She took a great deal of care of them, and gathered them under her wing every night, and fed them, and nursed them very well; and they were all very good, except two Cocks, that were always quarrelling with one another.*"

Emily made a clicking noise with her mouth, and, to Trefor's great amusement, was shaking her head with a very serious look on her face.

"They were not good where they?" He said

---

[1]. *Lessons for Children Part IV for Children from Three to Four Years Old. Mrs. Barbauld (Anna Letitia), 1798.*

before continuing to read. "*They were hardly out of their shell before they began to peck at each other...*"

Two stories later, Trefor closed the book. Emily was sleeping against his side, and the three other mobile children along with Miss Bennet were at his feet.

"You are very good at reading aloud," Miss Bennet said.

"So good that my audience has fallen asleep," he whispered in reply.

"Hand me the book."

Trefor placed the book in Miss Bennet's hands.

"Emily's cot is the one in the right corner," Martha said.

"You expect me to move her?" She was so little and looked so comfortable where she was.

"Unless you wish to stay there until she wakes up in an hour or so."

Trefor looked at the youngster beside him. She was adorable, but he was not certain he wished to remain here for an hour.

"Scoop her up being careful to keep her head from flopping. A flopping head will surely wake her." Martha had joined them. "Emily does not take kindly to being woken."

"Nor do I," Trefor said with a smile. Carefully, he slid one hand behind Emily's back and the other under her legs. Then, not daring to breathe, he lifted her to cradle her against his chest and pushed out of the rocker — which was harder to do than expected when one did not have any hands to assist in the motion.

"This cot?" he whispered when he had crossed the room.

Miss Bennet nodded.

"The blanket," he said. "How do I pull it back and not drop Emily?"

To his great relief, Miss Bennet came to his aid and soon Emily and her baby were snuggled beneath her covers.

"You performed admirably," Martha commended.

"You did," Miss Bennet agreed. "Why are you here?"

"To learn about children," he answered. "How am I to know if I like them if I do not spend any time with them? I wish to be better prepared should you ask me about them again at some point."

Miss Bennet, who had taken a spot on the floor

again, looked up at him in astonishment. "You are here because of me?"

He shrugged. "Yes." Spotting the blocks, he went to the shelf and retrieved them.

"For me?" Miss Bennet replied when he had returned to the rug and taken a seat next to a little fellow.

"No, these are for this young man." He looked at her. "What is his name?"

"That is Jack."

"Jack, would you like to build a castle?"

"I did not mean are the blocks for me," Miss Bennet said.

"You did not?"

She shook her head, her cheeks flushing. "I cannot believe you are here because of me."

"You pointed out a shortfall, and so it must be attended to." He turned his attention back to Jack who was twice the size of Emily. "Now, young Jack. Can you count to three? For we are going to stack them in rows like this. One, two, three." He handed a block to Jack. "Just here. One. Say one."

The child repeated what sounded like one, and so Trefor handed him another block. "Just on top.

Two. Say two. Ah, very good. Now, three, in just the same fashion."

"Why must they all be three high?" Miss Bennet said as she scooted closer to him.

"This is the wall, and the pediment shall be just behind it." He pulled out a soldier from the basket of blocks. "And our guards will stand so." He placed the soldier atop the blocks. "Two," he corrected Jack who had counted one, three.

He smiled at the young lad. "You know," he said to Kitty. "I think I might like children."

"You did think you would," she reminded him.

"Indeed, I did, and that is likely why I like them. After all, the proper attitude in approaching a matter is of great importance." He was quite pleased with himself. "Do you not think?" He turned to Miss Bennet.

"Yes." She smiled as her head bobbed up and down.

He loved how her face lit with her enjoyment. If there were not a child needing attention, he would have gladly admired her features for longer than a brief moment.

"One remembers how to play quite quickly, do they not?" he said.

"You had forgotten how to play?"

"I assure you I have not had my blocks out to build castles in years."

She giggled.

"But I must admit it is rather enjoyable." Tidy columns and rows, all nice and orderly, were very pleasant to build, even if they were eventually going to be knocked through.

"And you are very good at it." Her words were filled with laughter.

"I always was," he answered, feeling just as light as her laugh.

Chapter 14

"I had expected you to be upstairs," Mr. Gardiner said as he came into the sitting room. "Lottie was asking about Mr. Linton, again." Kitty's uncle chuckled. "When she takes a liking to someone, she is not easily persuaded away from it."

"He is coming to call tomorrow."

"I hope he will spare a minute or two for your cousin."

Kitty put down her pen. "I am certain he will." She remembered how sweet little Emily had looked tucked in beside Mr. Linton earlier today.

"I am happy to see you smiling when we speak of him rather than looking anxious as you have for the past three days."

Kitty shrugged but said nothing in explanation. She was not sure she could explain herself for she had still not sorted out her feelings where Mr. Linton was concerned. They were a puzzling mixture of longing and curiosity — and not just because he was handsome. She felt herself being drawn to him, to discover who he was beneath the face he presented to the world — much like discovering who Mr. L was beneath his tattered coat in her story. Neither Mr. Linton or his fictional counterpart were proving to be dreadful under their cover of initial disagreeableness.

"Do you have more of your story for me to read?"

Pulling her lower lip between her teeth, Kitty looked at her notebook. She was at a good stopping point. Mr. L had just completed his second test.

"I promise not to critique it too harshly." Her uncle gave her a pleading look. "But you had left Mr. L with two more tasks to complete. He had only just defeated the great beast and gotten the log he needed. I am anxious to see what trial befalls him next."

Kitty picked up her notebook. "He has just –"

"No. Do not tell me. Let me read it. Please."

"Is my husband begging for stories?" Aunt Gardiner said as she entered the room.

Kitty laughed. "He is, and I was just about to oblige him."

Mrs. Gardiner sucked in a quick breath as her face lit with excitement. "And may I read it after he does?"

Kitty shook her head as she laughed again. "Do you really wish to read it?" Or were they only being kind?

"More than I can say without looking very foolish," her aunt replied.

"But it is only my scribblings."

"Which makes them all the more precious," her aunt said. "What makes you look so astonished, my dear? Do you not expect me to love everything you do?"

Kitty once again shook her head slowly. A sheepish look settled on her face. "I am not Lizzy or Jane."

"Do they write stories?"

The smile her aunt wore said that the answer to such a question was already known, but Kitty answered anyway. "Not to my knowledge."

"Then, you might have to explain yourself a bit further."

"I think I know this answer," her uncle said

before Kitty could do more than open her mouth and begin to organize her thoughts. "Lizzy is bright, and Jane is so proper and good that it is hard not to think one must be those things to be well-thought of. Is that not right?"

"Yes, yes. That is very true," Kitty said. That was a great deal of the issue. How often had she heard one or the other of her sisters praised for such things? Too many to count!

"And is it too hard to believe that you could be either of those things?" her uncle asked.

"Well, yes, but that is not it entirely." That was indeed another piece which made her feel inadequate. But that was only because —

"Then, what is the rest?" Her uncle held her notebook on his lap, ignoring it as if what she had to say was much more important than the pleasure to be found in reading a much-anticipated portion of a story.

"I am," she looked down at her hands, for the rest was not easy to admit, "silly."

"Perhaps at times," her uncle said, "but then so is everyone."

"Not Jane or Lizzy!"

Her uncle chuckled. "Even Jane and Lizzy." He

winked at her before picking up the notebook he held.

Surely not!

"I assure you it is true," he replied in answer to her look of shock. "You know." He shifted his focus to the story he held. "I could read this aloud."

Oh, no! She could not sit here and listen to that!

"Please do," his wife cried. "You are an excellent reader."

"What say you, Kitty? May I?"

She looked between her aunt and uncle. They really were the best of people. They loved her despite her silliness, which they claimed was not so terrible as Papa seemed to declare. And at present, they both wore such eager expressions — much like Lottie did when she was awaiting a story. That, coupled with the fact that they had just been so kind to her in saying she was not silly, made it impossible for her to deny them. "Must I stay to listen?" she asked.

"Not if you do not wish to," her uncle said.

"Then, yes, you may read it aloud. However, I do not think I am equal to listening." She rose from her chair.

"Catherine."

She was beginning to like hearing herself called that by her uncle, for, while it might from time to time be followed by a gentle scold, whatever followed it was always said as if he thought her an equal and not a child.

"Thank you," he said when she turned toward him. "For sharing this with us." He held up the book.

A smile spread from her lips to her heart. "You are most welcome."

She ducked out of the room and closed the door until it almost latched. Then, she leaned against the wall next to the door and listened.

"*Several minutes later, Mr. L rounded a bend in the road, looking behind him to make certain that the beast was truly dead and not following him. To his immense relief, there was only path behind him and naught else.*

He put the log down and sat on it for a full five minutes. His legs burned from running and his breathing was labored. His arm that had been cut was growing cold and sore.

This path back to the village was longer than the way he had come, but it had seemed the best direction to escape from the beast. However..."

Kitty smiled. Her uncle was a very good reader,

and it was not so very dreadful to hear her words read by him. She pushed off the wall and moved toward the stairs. It was not right to listen at doors, even if one was listening to her own words. It was not proper, and in town, she was trying to be proper. For the past several days, she had achieved her goal. She had said what was proper, refrained from saying too much that was improper, and behaved as she thought a proper lady should. She had even managed to accomplish being proper at Mrs. Verity's today. And all this had happened despite Mr. Linton being present. Perhaps there was hope for them to be good friends, or maybe even more, if they could continue to meet without arguing.

She slipped into her room and sat quietly on her bed in the light of the lamp she had brought up from downstairs. Today had been a perfect day, and she was reluctant to have it end. However, after five minutes of watching the flame flicker, tiredness began to creep over her, and so, she rose and prepared for bed, taking extra care when deciding which dress she would wear tomorrow for callers.

Before climbing into bed, she placed that dress

next to the ball gown she would wear to tomorrow night. Then, with thoughts of dancing and tea mingling in her mind with blocks and children, she slid into her dreams which were filled with a tall, handsome fellow with the most perfect silvery grey eyes.

~*~*~

"You look beautiful." Elizabeth wrapped her arm around Kitty's. "I wish I was half as pretty."

Kitty's brow furrowed.

"You are becoming quite as pretty as Jane," Elizabeth whispered. "But do not tell her or Lydia I said so." She laughed.

"You truly think I am beautiful? Like Jane?"

"Oh, most certainly," Elizabeth assured her. "I will tell you something else, but you must promise me you will not be too startled."

"I will try to keep my composure," Kitty assured her eagerly. Elizabeth did not tell anyone secrets, save Jane. Well, perhaps she also told Mr. Darcy now, but before she was married, she only ever told her secrets to Jane.

"Mr. Darcy and I are quite impressed by the fine young lady you are becoming. Even in the face of disaster, you have done quite well. I am not certain

I could glide into this ballroom with the grace with which you have tonight. There is almost an elegance about you which makes me think you are no longer my little sister, but a wonderful lady I know."

"You are teasing me." There was no way that she fit Elizabeth's description. Her stomach was twisting, her heartbeat was as quick as if she had been dancing already, and her thoughts whispered doubts that she might do or say something which would be her ruin.

"No, I assure you I am not," Elizabeth said. "You are different here compared to at home. I can see why Mr. Linton is so taken with you."

"Please, I am not as you say." Kitty would also like to refute that Mr. Linton was taken with her, but he had declared her beautiful in front of Elizabeth, Mr. Darcy, and Aunt Gardiner. So, there was no way she could honestly deny it. Nor could she truthfully wish to be able to deny it.

"You are." Elizabeth gave her a firm glare.

"Thank you." What else did one say to such a thing when she neither wished to start an argument or provoke Lizzy into scolding her?

"And there is Mr. Linton now." Elizabeth

sounded nearly as excited as Mama might about a potential match for Jane. "Remember, you and he are to dance two sets."

Kitty nodded her understanding and sucked in a quick breath when she saw him. He was wearing dark blue. Goodness! He looked handsome in dark blue.

"Miss Bennet," he greeted with a bow, "are you ready to make one and all believe we are happily courting?"

"As long as you do not provoke me." She fluttered her lashes and smiled coyly just as Lydia would do when she was attempting to sway a gentleman to like her. Kitty gasped.

"Are you well?" Mr. Linton asked.

"Perfectly," she hurried to reply as her cheeks grew warm. "I just was thinking. It was nothing." Nothing that was going to make her feel at ease that is.

Why had she fluttered her lashes at Mr. Linton? They were friends. One did not flirt with a friend.

However, her brow furrowed, they were supposed to appear to be more than friends. She smiled. That was it. She was just playing her part so well that she did not need to think about it. Unless…

No, it was not because she was enamoured with him. Was it?

"Do you still wish to dance?" He was looking utterly befuddled.

"Most assuredly."

She would need to put startling thoughts out of her head. For each time she and Mr. Linton had met where he looked confused had not ended well.

"Truly forgive me for woolgathering." She took his hand. "The room is splendid; is it not?"

"Indeed, Mrs. Belmont is known to host an excellent ball. It is her second this season. The first made the papers."

He was wearing a smirk that begged her to ask if there was some pleasant memory from that ball that caused him to look amused, and so she asked.

"You will likely think me horrid if I tell you," he replied.

Again, his lips lifted in a teasing smirk. It was almost as if he were flirting with her! But gentlemen such as Mr. Linton did not flirt; did they?

"I promise not to think you are horrid," she assured him as she took her place across from him.

"My sister nearly ended up married to Mr. Edwards after that particular ball."

The first notes of *Strawberries and Cream* were played, and Kitty's curiosity about what Mr. Linton had said was left to fester and grow as she wound her way through the dance, swaying side to side, hopping, turning, crossing, and returning through the line as required.

"You must tell me more," she said at one point when she actually had a moment to speak when they joined hands.

"I will." He parted from her again. It was many steps later before he could reply further. "Perhaps a walk in the garden?"

"Oh, yes," she said before they were once again parted.

Some dances provided more chances to speak. She scowled wishing that this was one of them — no matter how invigoratingly delightful she found the patterns. Indeed, she was to be frustrated by dancing for the rest of the set, as well as two others, before she finally found herself on Mr. Linton's arm and strolling through the small garden.

She glanced back toward the terrace where Lizzy stood with Mr. Darcy. Their presence gave approval to Kitty's wandering the paths with Mr. Linton, while lanterns stood tall along the side of the path, providing ample light. The breeze was cool, but not too cold. However, if they remained outside for too long, she was going to wish she had worn her shawl as her sister had suggested.

"There are a few alcoves on your way to the retiring room," Mr. Linton said.

"Yes, I noticed them. They have lovely red drapes."

"That hide a couple quite nicely, or so I hear," Mr. Linton's steps faltered.

"I suppose they would. They did look as if they would be a pleasant place to find some solitude and quiet."

"Solitude and quiet are not precisely why a couple might seek out such a place."

He was using that tone of voice which seemed to be very natural for him to use. It was the one that sounded a great deal like a tutor, instructing his students on the best way to do something.

"I do know that," she said, looking up at him. "However, I did not think it would be best if I mentioned any other activities." She fluttered her lashes and smiled.

"Right, right. Forgive me." He sighed. "Would you mind not looking at me?"

Kitty's brow furrowed. "I do not see why I cannot look at you. Is there something wrong with how I do it?"

"No, no. There is most certainly nothing wrong with how you look. In fact, it is quite the opposite which is the problem."

"You make very little sense at times," Kitty muttered, a small pout forming on her lips.

"I would have to agree."

"You would?"

"Yes. Now, please mind your steps so that I can speak without becoming any more turned about than I am."

Kitty giggled. "Am I being vexing again, Mr. Linton. I promise I had not meant to be."

"Vexing, unsettling, alluring, tempting." He blew out a breath. "Perhaps we should return to the house before I forget myself entirely."

"You have not told me your story. We cannot go back until I know how your sister nearly became betrothed to Mr. Edwards at a ball which was held here."

"She met with him in one of those alcoves –

not by herself, mind you. Miss Barrett was with her, but the gossips do not always care about the details. To make a long story short, the incident found its way to the paper, and I stormed off to demand that Edwards marry her."

"Did she not tell you the story was wrong?" She could not imagine that he would not listen to his sister.

"She did." He paused and chuckled to himself as if thinking. It was a rather disparaging sound. "Perhaps I should have listened to her and not sought out Mr. Edwards, but a reputation is a fragile thing. How could I, as her brother and guardian, allow her reputation to be destroyed. There was only one way to save her from disgrace, or so I thought." Again, he made a small disparaging chuckle sound. "However, I was wrong, and it all ended with Connie happily betrothed to Mr. Crawford, which, before that story in the paper, was what I had hoped to have happen."

"You did?" Kitty was feeling rather confused. "Was not Mr. Crawford a rake like Mr. Edwards?"

"He was until he decided not to be and, against my wishes, sought help in affecting his change from my sister."

Kitty stopped walking. "Wait. You did not wish for your sister to help him, but you then wished for her to marry him?"

Mr. Linton nodded.

"You are perplexing."

"Let me explain," he said. "When I first heard of Connie's willingness to help Crawford, I feared she would lose her heart to him, which she did, and then, once it was lost, of course, my hopes had to be that it would not be broken."

That part was understandable, but... "Yet, you were going to make her marry Mr. Edwards?"

"Her reputation..." he said with a shrug.

Kitty shook her head. "I would have talked to Mr. Crawford and asked him to offer for her."

"As Mr. Darcy did of me?"

Kitty laughed lightly. Mr. Linton was looking at her rather intensely, and she wondered if he realized how unsettling such a look was capable of making him be.

"I suppose it is rather the same, except we are only courting," she leaned closer and lowered her voice, "or pretending to be."

"I'd very much like it if we were not pretending," he said. "Indeed, I wish we were not courting."

Kitty stepped backward. Her heart stung as if it had been slapped. "Well, I can break our arrangement at any time. You only need to tell me that you do not wish to continue. I am sure I shall not care one jot if you do." Except that she would, and the tears in her eyes were surely giving away her lie.

He grasped her hand. "That is not what I meant. It is not that I do not wish to court you. It is that I wish to," his mouth dropped open as a furrow formed between his eyes.

"You wish to what?" Kitty prodded. Such a look of surprise and bewilderment on a gentleman's face was far too tantalizing to a curious lady such as herself.

"Marry you?"

There was nearly as much question in his voice as there was in her mind. It was as if the idea was as utterly new and disquieting to him as it was to her.

"We have known each other only a short time," she managed to say after a moment of staring at him with her mouth agape and a million thoughts, many of them startling, running through her mind.

"You are right," he said quickly. "It makes no sense. I am sure it must just be the lantern light and the music."

She saw his throat move up and down.

"And your enchanting eyes and the flowers in your hair." Hesitantly, he touched her cheek. "I do not understand it," he whispered.

Such a soft touch both by his fingers and his words was intoxicating. Kitty felt herself slipping from the garden in which she knew she stood to some other place that was filled with stars which shone like precious jewels and with warm breezes that caressed and soothe one's soul. And then, in a moment, she was plopped back in the garden as Mr. Linton, stepped away from her, leaving her feeling bereft.

His chest was rising and falling deliberately. "We should go back." His voice was strained.

"We should?"

"Straight away," he said with a nod.

"Why?" She really did not wish to leave this place, this feeling of something she did not understand but craved.

He stepped closer to her again. "Because if we do not, I will likely kiss you, and then, you will have no choice but to marry me."

"And that is bad?" Her mind should know the answer to this. A compromise was never a good thing, and yet, at this moment, it seemed anything but bad.

"It is." He cupped her cheek in his hand. "I could never force you to do what you do not wish."

"And if I wish it?" Did she? Was that for what she longed? Was the ache in her chest the result of wishing for him to ask her to marry him and him not doing so? Did she love him?

He shook his head, his eyes filling with sadness as his thumb caressed her cheek. "You do not wish it. It is the garden and the lanterns' light."

"That is rather disappointing." Excessively so. "Are you certain it is not your eyes? They are the loveliest mixture of blue and silver."

He smiled. "I am almost certain it should be more than even my eyes or your beauty that precipitates a marriage. Although, you are unsettling so I could be wrong." He shook his head once more and stepped back. "We should wait until we know for certain, do you not think?"

She shrugged but put her hand on his proffered arm. "If it is what you wish and think is best."

"Best, yes. What I wish?" He shook his head. "It is most certainly not what I wish."

It seemed, Kitty thought as they began walking

back toward the terrace, that she and Mr. Linton finally agreed on something, for returning to the house was also certainly not what she wished. And that was indeed unsettling — deliciously so.

Chapter 15

"You are in the paper again," Charles Edwards dropped into a chair at the table where Trefor sat in their club.

"Yes, I saw."

"Is that why Darcy is glaring at you?"

Trefor turned toward the far corner of the room. "He is not glaring at me. He is looking nowhere in particular."

Edwards! Always attempting to stir up trouble. It was a good thing his sister was marrying Henry and not Edwards. Miss Barrett and her mother were far better equipped with the sternness and resolve needed to deal with the likes of Edwards.

Charles smirked. "You'd be glaring."

"No, I would not." He leveled a harsh look at his friend. "You should know."

Edwards leaned back in his chair, completely

unaffected by either Trefor's look or words. But then, that was how Charles was. It should not surprise him. Trefor finished the last of his cup of tea and rose.

"Where are you going? I just arrived," Charles said.

"To speak to Darcy."

Edward's eyes grew wide. "Indeed?" Rising, he followed along behind Trefor.

"Darcy," Trefor greeted as he reached where the man was sitting.

"Linton." Darcy folded his paper and placed it on the table. "I was wondering how long it would be before you came to see me." He motioned for Trefor to take a seat. "I am meeting a friend here, but I do not expect him to be on time. He rarely is."

"Is that so?" Edwards asked.

"Quite," Darcy replied. "Bingley follows his own schedule. Neither the sun nor a watch is going to dictate his plans." He chuckled. "That is not entirely true. He intends to be on time. It just never seems to happen." Darcy took a sip of his tea. "There is always someone to speak to on his way."

"A friendly sort is he?" Edwards asked.

"Very." Darcy took another sip of his tea. "His

wife is my wife's sister. They have not seen each other since we married over two months ago, so we men are letting them get reacquainted without us." His lips tipped into a smile. "Especially since they intend to spend their time together visiting some new shop that is opening today."

"Durward, Waller, and Eldridge," Trefor said with a nod.

"That is the very one."

"I am on my way there as soon as Crawford arrives. He is collecting my sister and aunt before he comes here. Crawford's sister is marrying Durward, and since Crawford is marrying my sister, it is imperative that we show our support, or so my aunt says." Trefor shrugged. "I suppose she is correct."

"It seems logical," Darcy agreed. "My wife's other sister will be there as well."

Trefor nodded as his ears grew warm. "I know. She told me."

Miss Bennet was the reason he was happy to do as his aunt suggested and visit the shop on its opening day. He even intended to spend some money on something in the shop if he could discover something that Miss Bennet would like.

"The gossips will surely have a grand time with that bit of news should they see you with her," Darcy said. "They are already enjoying themselves judging by the account in the paper." His left brow rose. "I did not see any amorous actions from the terrace last night."

"There were none." Trefor was not about to admit to having caressed Kitty's cheek to Mr. Darcy. If the man had not seen it, he did not need to know about it.

"She did seem not quite herself after your walk." Trefor's brow furrowed. "How so?"

"She was more distracted than normal and did a lot of smiling and sighing." The gentleman's lips pursed as if attempting not to laugh. It seemed that Mr. Darcy took great pleasure in causing Trefor to feel uneasy.

"You do not know the reason for that, do you?" Darcy asked, causing Edwards to chuckle.

"No," Trefor lied. He was nearly certain that he knew the reason.

"Indeed?" There was no little amount of disbelief in Darcy's voice.

Trefor shook his head.

"No idea whatsoever?" Darcy prodded.

Again, Trefor shook his head.

"Out with it, Linton," Edwards said as he gave Trefor's arm a jab. "Not even you can be so clueless as to not know if something said on a garden stroll caused a lady to be distracted. What was it? Did you confess your undying love?"

"No," Trefor snapped.

"Did you propose marriage?" Edwards asked with a laugh that fell silent when Trefor did not reply. "You did not? Did you?"

Trefor shrugged. "No, although the word might have come up in conversation."

"You talked about marrying?" Darcy leaned forward.

Trefor shook his head. "I did not intend to. I had not even thought I wished to marry her until..." He shrugged again. "Until it came out of my mouth. I honestly do not know what is wrong with me. I do not blurt things. I do not almost kiss ladies at balls. My name does not appear in the paper."

Edwards grasped his shoulder, turning Trefor toward him. "Did you almost kiss her again?"

"No."

Edwards grinned. "But you wanted to. I can see it in your eyes."

"You see nothing of the sort," Trefor snapped.

"Convince her to marry you," Darcy said. "There is no other option."

"Do you really think so? The article in the paper did not seem so bad as all that to me. A push towards it perhaps but not something which would require it," Trefor said.

Darcy shook his head. "I am not speaking about the paper. Trust me when I say I know of what I speak." He smiled. "I tried to avoid marrying my wife."

"Do tell," Edwards was once again leaning back in his chair looking for all the world like there was nothing more important than the weather being discussed.

"Suffice it to say, my sister was good enough to push me in the right direction," Darcy said. "Which is what I am now attempting to do for you. If you love her, do not let her go."

Love. That was the thing about which Trefor had been thinking since that moment in the garden. How did one know if one was merely attracted to a lady or in love? He wished to ask someone but to do so felt so foolish. It was something he thought he should know. He had been able to see it in his sister. Why was he not able to see it for himself?

He was still pondering this thought when he entered Durward's store. And he likely would have continued thinking about it, if it had not been for seeing *her* standing at a case next to her aunt, exclaiming about something. As soon as he was able, he moved in her direction. However, by the time he reached where she had been, she had moved.

The store was busy. There were customers at every display case. Many were having parcels wrapped while others were deliberating over a purchase while the shop assistant stood waiting to either wrap up the purchase or put the item back on display.

Crawford's sister was marrying a shrewd businessman from the look of this store and the brisk business being conducted. She would likely never want for anything.

Finally, it was his turn to speak to the man behind the display case. "There was a young lady here who seemed taken by some item in this display just a moment ago."

"If I am thinking of the same lady," the shop

assistant said, "she was looking at this lace." He placed a length of lace on top of the case.

Lace. Of course, Trefor thought with chuckle. They had discussed lace once, although discussed was perhaps not the best choice of words. He had offended her over lace. "It is lovely."

"It is large enough to wrap around one's shoulders on a fine spring day. It would most certainly set off the lady's features."

That was true. Miss Bennet would look lovely wearing it.

"She seemed to think that this brooch would be just the thing to keep it in place."

"A young lady with hazel eyes and brown hair who was just here with her aunt?"

"She was with Mrs. Gardiner," the assistant said. "There was something in the back that caught Mrs. Gardiner's ear, and so they left to see to that without completing the purchase."

"I will take them both. If you would wrap them up and tell me the total."

"Immediately, sir. I will not be long."

"I will just wander this direction and return. I promise to not leave without that parcel." Trefor wandered toward the back of the store, looking in one case after another and stopping to admire the tea caddies.

The door to the back was open. Not fully, but halfway. Trefor moved to look through to the hall beyond, hoping to see Miss Bennet. She was there, but the sight made his heart lurch.

Turning away, he went back to the case to wait for his purchase to be wrapped. Who was that gentleman and why was Miss Bennet holding his hands? And why was her aunt allowing such an intimate gesture?

He placed his money on the counter. "Will you see that Miss Bennet gets this?" They were for her. No matter what he had witnessed. No matter if her heart belonged to another.

"Was there a name to tell her?"

Trefor shook his head. "Just a friend who thinks she has an excellent eye for lace of high quality."

"Very well, sir. I will tell her."

With a nod and a thank you, Trefor parted from the man.

"Where are you going?" his aunt asked when he passed her on his way toward the door.

He closed his eyes at the frustration of being stopped in his escape. "Outside."

"Is something amiss?"

"No." He moved toward the door.

"Trefor," his aunt hurried to follow him.

"Please, Aunt Gwladys," he said. "I am just not in the right frame of mind to enjoy this little adventure." Although, in that brief moment of seeing Miss Bennet standing so close to another gentleman while engaged in what looked like a serious conversation, his world, which had been set on akilter upon his first meeting with Miss Bennet, had righted itself before crumbling at his feet.

"Are you going home?"

"Eventually."

Aunt Gwladys put her hand on his arm. "Are you well?"

"I just need some air." And to be far away from here. "It is a bit stuffy in here."

His aunt's brow furrowed. "How are you getting home?"

"I will walk the street for a few minutes, and then, if possible, I will take a hack if you and Connie are not finished."

"We planned to make one more stop on our way home," his aunt cautioned. "But you could sit in the carriage. We have Henry to escort us."

How he wished he had ridden his horse. A ride through the park would be just the thing. "I think I shall take a hack and then go for a ride when I get home."

"In the park?"

He nodded. "Rotten Row," he said before ducking out of the store. He looked up the street and then down before deciding on a direction.

An hour later, he was feeling no less agitated, despite the pleasure of riding.

Love. He scoffed at the notion. It was a tricky fellow this thing called love. Skirting the room, poking at the occupants, disguising itself as attraction and friendship, hiding itself in a laugh, peeking out of a pair of fine eyes, but never fully revealing himself until he stood ready to rend a heart in two and dispose of the pieces. Why anyone sought such a thing as love was at this moment beyond his understanding. And he had no desire to attempt to understand it. He knew enough. With any luck, his heart would heal and not be utterly destroyed, though he suspected it might be too late for such a wish.

Tomorrow or the next day, the papers would carry his name again in a story. This time he would not be the gent hopeful of acceptance but rather the one who had been spurned. There was no need to continue with the charade of courting when Miss Bennet's affections lay elsewhere.

He stopped and dismounted, choosing to lean against a tree as he watched others driving past in their carriages — happy couples tempting love to show his darkness.

He laughed bitterly and closed his eyes, revisiting the scene in the back of Durward's store and feeling the disappointment which threatened to crush him. It was best to get such melancholy thoughts out of the way before he returned home to his questioning aunt and sister.

"What did you think you were doing?" a familar and angry voice penetrated his troubling thoughts.

His eyes popped open. A carriage was stopped in front of him. It was his own carriage with the canopy lowered, driven by Henry and containing his sister, his aunt, and a much displeased Miss Bennet.

"I was taking a moment to enjoy this tree before continuing my ride."

Miss Bennet glared at him. "Mr. Crawford, if you would be so kind as to help me out of the carriage. I would rather not yell at Mr. Linton from here."

With a laugh, Crawford, the wretched traitor, immediately offered his assistance.

"How might I be of service?" Trefor eyed her suspiciously as she approached him.

"You can tell me what you thought you were doing." She folded her arms and glared at him.

"I already did."

"Not now." She huffed as if he were being difficult, which he was not – not intentionally at any rate.

"Then, when?"

"You bought me a gift?"

Oh!

"Was it not right? I can see if we can exchange it for something else."

She stamped her foot. "It was perfect!"

His brow furrowed. "Then, I do not understand the issue."

"You cannot just give a lady a gift and leave without allowing her to either accept it or not."

"If you do not want it, I will take it back."

She huffed again. "I do not not want it."

"Then, you are accepting it?"

"Yes." If exasperation had a face, it was Miss Bennet's, although Trefor was not sure why she was exasperated. She seemed to know what she was talking about which was a great deal more than what he knew.

He shook his head. "I do not understand," he said apologetically.

"You left."

"I did not think you would notice."

Her look of exasperation changed to one of perturbation. "Why would you think that?"

"I saw you."

Her brow furrowed.

"And him," Trefor added. "Whomever he is. You looked rather cozy, holding hands and standing so close."

Her brow remained furrowed.

"In the back hall of the store," he explained. "Some tall, handsome chap."

"Of all the stupid things," she spat. "You, Mr. Linton are provoking and excessively vexing and..." She stamped her foot before moving closer to him. "And stupid. You do not know what you saw, yet you assume that I am the sort of lady who goes around cozying up to every handsome fellow."

"No, no. I did not think that. I just thought your uncle owns the building, and so you might have met this gentleman before and had..." he shrugged, "lost your heart to him, but you could not tell me just yet since you know there was that letter and the pretending to court thing." He looked down. "I could not stay and see you happy with him."

"Why?" her eyes were wide.

He searched her face for any sign of understanding, but there was none. "Do you truly not know?"

She smiled at him, softly, in the most becoming fashion, and then said, "yes" gently, just as she might to Emily or Jack in the nursery at Mrs. Verity's. Such a response told him that there was understanding behind her look of surprise from just moments ago. He longed to be given the years he knew he likely needed to discover how to read her expressions and understand her way of thinking.

"My heart would not survive it," he explained. "It is barely holding together as it is."

She stepped closer to him, tears gathering in her eyes. "That is how my heart feels."

"It is?" Hope leapt within him as she nodded.

"Do you think," she paused and tipped her head,

"do you think we might now know what we did not know last night?"

"Is there any way you can speak plainly?" he begged. He was not capable of deciphering much of anything presently. Hope and joy clung to the edges of his mind, waiting either to be allowed entrance or to be dashed to the ground.

"Do you not remember saying you wished to marry me?"

Oh, that he remembered. He stepped so that he was less than an arm's length away from her.

"And I thought I might wish the same." Her voice was only just louder than a whisper.

"And do you?" He sucked in a breath and waited.

"I am mostly certain I do." She fluttered her lashes and smiled at him. Did she know just how tempting she was when she did such a thing?

"Mostly certain?"

She shrugged. "I suppose you could kiss me, and then, I would have no choice but to be completely certain."

"That is a rather scandalous option," he cautioned. "There would be no changing your mind."

She smiled. "It makes no sense, you know. You

are impossibly annoying, and I have only known you for a short time. However," she shook her head. "It is just ridiculous. It is likely too foolish."

He nodded. "You are right. There are those who would say it is. How can I love you when I know so very little about you?"

"Precisely!" she agreed. "I should not love you so soon. It is not how it is done, you know." Her forehead wrinkled. "Except my sister Jane assured me that it is not impossible because she loved Mr. Bingley from the first time she danced with him."

"I have heard that it happens," he agreed as he took her hands, "though I thought it only happened to less logical people than me." She was smiling at him as if he had missed something. But what was it? Oh! Yes. "You love me?"

She nodded. "I do. You are a good man with a noble heart."

"And lovely eyes," he added with a smirk.

"Yes, perfectly lovely eyes." She stepped a fraction of a step closer to him as if she felt the same pull that he did.

"And under all your provoking vexingness," he said, "you are just the sort of lady I need, for you see things as I do not, and you are genuine. There is no artifice in you. And your heart..." He pulled her into his embrace. He knew he should not, but he was powerless to resist the compulsion to hold her. "The care contained in your heart shines through your eyes and displays itself in your actions. Will you, Miss Bennet, allow me the chance to get to know you better and better for the rest of our lives?"

"As husband and wife?" She fluttered her lashes at him again.

"Yes, my provoking love. Will you be my wife?"

"Considering the scandal you are creating by holding me as you are, I think I must." She made no move to extricate herself from his embrace and instead, placed a hand on his cheek. "But I submit to my destiny happily. It is a most willing surrender."

Then, with a whispered *I love you* from one to the other, they sealed their union and their future with a kiss that was as pure as it was passionate, stirring desires and mingling souls as only love of the truest sort, which inspires tales of brave quests to break curses, can do. And there, in the park, on the edge of Rotten Row, on a fine spring day, a gentleman, who was a stranger to scandal, and a lady, who was bent on being proper in town, inspired yet another story for the society pages that would keep the gossips' tongues wagging for some time as they whispered behind fans and smiled over teacups, sharing their version of this delicious scandal in springtime.

Before You Go

If you enjoyed this book, be sure to let others know by leaving a review.

~*~*~

Would you like to read the story that Kitty wrote about Mr. L?

Or, do you want to know when the next Leenie B book will be available?

You can do both when you sign up to my mailing list.

Book News from Leenie Brown

(bit.ly/LeenieBBookNews)

~*~*~

Turn the page to read an excerpt of another one of Leenie's books

His Inconvenient
Choice Excerpt

If you enjoy stories about Kitty Bennet, you might enjoy His Inconvenient Choice, the third book in my Choices series, in which Kitty and Colonel Fitzwilliam struggle to find a way to be together despite Lord Matlock's objections.

CHAPTER 1

January 1, 1812

Colonel Richard Fitzwilliam unfolded the small piece of paper that had been tucked into his pocket as he left Netherfield after the wedding breakfast. He shook his head. Two cousins and a friend married all within the space of two weeks was enough to set anyone's world on end. It was also the sort of thing that made him contemplate his own future. Such thoughts often made his breathing feel forced. He drew a deep breath, trying to rid his body of the feeling of being crushed, but it was only slightly helpful. He knew that his future was not to be so happy as those of his cousins and Bingley. He was not free to choose where he wished. His marriage would be one of convenience; his father would see to that.

He looked surreptitiously at the paper in his palm, not wishing to draw attention to it from the others in the carriage. The drawing there brought a smile to his lips and a pang of regret to his heart. Forget-me-nots graced the lid of a box from which spilled strands of pearls and chains of gold. He folded the drawing again and slipped it back into his pocket. If his heart could make his choice for him instead of his father, Kitty Bennet would be his choice. She had stolen his heart when she shivered in the wind on the street in front of the milliner's shop as she insisted on being introduced to him as Katherine. Upon further acquaintance, she had proven to be a lady who shared many of his same interests and who made him feel at ease. She expected no more from him than to be himself. He did not need to be a military leader or the son of an earl. She was interested in his wooden creations — and not as a lady who was trying to make a favourable impression on a gentleman. No, she listened with interest and animation. She had even sketched a few designs that he might like to use.

"If you could wait but a year," she had said as they strolled the perimeter of the ballroom last evening, "then your inheritance would be yours."

"He will not allow me to be free. He will insist on my marrying before he gives me one farthing more than I have," he had replied. Her eyes had filled with tears that she refused to shed, and his heart had broken a bit more at the thought of a life without her. "If I could wait," he had whispered, "I would wait a thousand years for you."

She had smiled sadly at him and said, "And I would wait for you."

He ran his gloved finger over the drawing in the pocket of his coat. "Do not forget me," she had said as she had slipped it into his pocket when he was taking his leave of her. He knew he would never forget her. His hand closed around the paper.

"You are looking rather pensive, Colonel," said Caroline Bingley. "Are they pleasant thoughts?"

"Not all of them," he said as he turned to look

out the window. If the weather had not been so foul, he would have refused Hurst's offer to travel with him.

"That is a pity," said Louisa. "I prefer to think on pleasant things whenever possible."

"As do I," said Richard, "but it is not always possible."

"A colonel must have many unpleasant things to consider," added Caroline.

"He must," said Richard. "However, I was not thinking as a colonel but as a mere man."

Hurst snorted at the comment. "Do leave him be, Caroline."

"I was only attempting to pass the time in conversation," she replied with a huff. "The light is too poor for anything else."

"I find a quiet nap a most refreshing way to pass a trip," replied Hurst.

"How dull," said Caroline.

"Not at all," said Richard. "I find I would like to close my eyes. It has been a busy two days."

Hurst nodded. "You were out with your men yesterday, were you not?"

"I put them through a few drills to test them. Those who passed were allowed to attend the ball.

Those who did not pass were confined to quarters for the evening." It had been his plan, and a successful one, to keep Wickham from the ball. He would take every opportunity afforded him by his position to ensure that Wickham had less pleasure than he desired. It was the one pleasure he received from his duty.

"And, I believe, you danced every dance, did you not?" asked Louisa.

"All save one." His heart pinched, for that one had been set aside to stroll with Kitty.

"Oh, Hurst, you are right. I do believe a nap must be had. What with an early morning yesterday for the colonel, a night of dancing, and another early start to the day today, he must be very tired." She turned to Caroline. "It would be unkind of us to keep him from his rest."

"I thank you," said Richard with a bow of his head. Then added, "I am indeed rather tired," as he settled back and closed his eyes.

Conversation with anyone at present would be unpleasant; with Caroline Bingley, it would be even more so. His fingers once again sought that slip of paper in his pocket. Finding it, he allowed his mind to wander to the lady who had given it to him, and with a deep exhale, he attempted to find some peace in sleep.

~*~*~

"Mr. Darcy, might I have a word with you?" Kitty turned from the window where she had been watching the Hursts' carriage drive away. There were not many wedding guests remaining, and she knew that both she and the Darcys would leave soon.

"Certainly," replied Darcy. He had not had very many opportunities to speak with Kitty. She seemed to avoid him whenever possible, and so her request surprised him. He watched her twist her fingers together and bite her lip, signs that he had learned through watching his wife indicated she was nervous.

"I have a little bit of money and expect to receive some more." She resisted the urge to duck her head and hide from him. His presence had always unsettled her. She was sure he was at any moment going to scold her for some foolishness. She knew she had no reason to feel so, but she did. However, she also knew that he would best be able to advise her, and so she straightened her shoulders and continued. "I have sold some designs to Mrs. Havelston, and she has requested some more. I have not signed them with my name, and it is to be a secret arrangement." The words rushed from her. "I would like to invest it. I know that you can earn money with money, but I do not know how to do it, and I am not a gentleman, which limits me."

He smiled at her. "That sounds like a wise thing to do."

Her brows drew together. "It does?"

"Indeed." He smiled at her again and was rewarded with a small smile in return.

She withdrew a small velvet pouch from her reticule. "It is really very little. It may not be enough to invest yet, but I dare not place it in my father's strongbox, for if something happens to him, I do not wish to explain it to Mr. Collins."

Darcy took the bag from her and slipped it into his pocket. "I shall care for it. You will keep a record of what you have given me, and I will do the same. You know how to do this?"

She pursed her lips and drew her brows together. "I will have my father show me."

"Very good."

"Mr. Darcy, could we save some time and trouble if I request my uncle to give the money to you?"

She twisted her hands again. "He regularly receives payments from Mrs. Havelston for her orders, so no one would suspect she is paying me if she gives it to him. And if he meets with you, no one would question the activity."

He nodded. The thought she had put into her plans impressed him. If he were perfectly honest with himself, he would not have thought her capable of such well-thought-out plans. She had, on the occasions when he had been in her company before his marriage to Elizabeth, struck him as flighty and silly. He chided himself. He had not noted such behaviour since their arrival last week. "I understand. This is an arrangement that is to be private."

"Very. If anyone was to learn that I was earning money..."

"I understand," said Darcy. "Do you have a plan in mind for the money?"

The tears that had been threatening all morning sprang to her eyes, and her cheeks flushed in embarrassment.

"You do not have to tell me," Darcy said quietly.

She shook her head. "I have a foolish notion that will probably be unsuccessful, but your cousin should not be forced to give up what he loves. I thought perhaps I could help him find a way to be happy." She shrugged. "If not, then the money can be added to my portion, which will be of assistance to me when I need to set up my own establishment. I do not wish to live solely on the charity of my relations."

"You do not plan to marry?" Darcy asked in some surprise.

The tears once again gathered in her eyes, and she blinked against them as she shook her head. "I had hoped," she said softly.

His eyes followed her gaze toward the window and the drive at Netherfield. "One must not lose hope, Miss Kitty. Circumstances can change."

She drew a deep breath and released it slowly as she steadied her emotions. Then, she gave him as much of smile as she could manage. "While I own that it is not an utter impossibility, I think it highly unlikely."

He nodded as she thanked him and went to join her father, who was saying his farewells to Elizabeth and Jane. Elizabeth caught Darcy's eye and gave him a questioning look and in response, he shrugged and smiled.

"You look troubled, my dear," she said as she slipped her arm into his and waved to her father's carriage.

"I believe I am," he said as he assisted her into their carriage. Then, he gave one more wave to Bingley and climbed in beside her. Shaking the rain from his hat, he set it on the bench across from them before tucking a blanket across their laps. "Shall we pass the journey as we did on our wedding day?"

She giggled. "I should like that very much, Mr. Darcy, but not until you tell me what has you troubled. I shall not be distracted by your sweet kisses until I know all."

"Is that a fact?" He leaned over and kissed her softly.

She smiled and pushed at his chest. "I would like nothing better than to be distracted so pleasantly, sir, but I am afraid my mind will not be settled until you have told me about what you and Kitty were speaking."

He gave her a quick kiss before she could stop him. "Very well. Your sister has asked me to help her with her finances. It seems she has sold some designs and intends to sell some more, and she wishes to have her earnings invested."

"And this has you troubled?" Elizabeth's brows furrowed as one eyebrow rose in disbelief. "Is it that she is earning money which has concerned you?"

He chuckled and shook his head. "Her selling designs and wishing to invest is not what has me troubled. I asked her what she intended to do with the money, and she nearly cried." He stroked Elizabeth's cheek with his thumb and smiled sadly at her. "Based on her answers and my cousin's strange behaviour last night and this morning, I believe she has had her heart broken by my uncle." He first gave Elizabeth's pursed lips a kiss and then the deep furrow between her brows. "She wishes to help Richard with her money. She does not wish to see him forced to give up what he loves. She also said she no longer intends to marry." He wrapped his arms around Elizabeth and drew her closer as he saw sadness enter her eyes. "And that has me troubled, for I do not wish to see either her or Richard give up whom they love."

"What can be done?" Elizabeth peeked up at him from where her head rested on his shoulder.

"I do not know. My uncle will make it challenging. He wishes a marriage of advantage for Richard, one that will strengthen his political ties and increase Richard's wealth. It will take some thought. However, nothing can be done at present." He kissed her forehead again. "And now, Mrs. Darcy, since I have told you all that is troubling me, I believe I may now distract you with kisses."

She wrapped her arms around his neck. "I believe you must." And eagerly, he obliged.

~*~*~

Richard handed his hat and coat to Harrison, the Matlocks' butler, and slipped into his mother's sitting room to greet her.

Lady Matlock held him close for a moment. "I am happy to see you safely returned to me. Will you be staying?" She took a seat on a settee and motioned for him to join her.

"I have no choice. I do not wish to impose on Darcy or Rycroft as they are settling in with their wives."

"There is BayLeafe," his mother said softly. BayLeafe was the small estate just outside of town which was part of the inheritance that should come to him through his mother should his father see fit to give it him.

He shook his head at her offering.

"Your father is in quite a state what with both of your cousins marrying outside of what is proper." She reached up and brushed his hair back from his forehead. "He is not all bad, you know. He has been good to me. He is just set in his ways."

"Do you love him?" Richard's voice was soft.

"I suppose I do," she replied. "It is possible to become friends and then more even when you begin as near strangers." She took his hand. "I cannot say I have never wished for more or for another, for I did at first, but now, I cannot imagine my life in any other way."

Richard nodded and placed the small folded drawing in her hand. "You would have liked her," he said as she unfolded the paper. Where his father blustered, his mother spoke softly. Where his father was arrogant, she demonstrated grace and humility. They were in many ways as opposed as darkness and light.

She lay the drawing on her lap, a hand resting on her heart. "It is very well done. Who is she?"

He shook his head and took the paper from her

lap. "It matters not, for it shall never be." He rose and went to the window. "She has neither wealth nor significant connections beyond our family."

Lady Matlock came to stand near him. "She is connected to our family?"

He nodded. "Her sisters are the new Mrs. Darcy and Lady Rycroft." He turned toward her. "And that is not the worst of it. A third sister is the new Mrs. Bingley." He watched her struggle with how to accept this information. He knew she loved him and would wish him only to be happy, but she also held to some of the same ideas regarding marriage as her husband. It was not only his father who wished him to make a good match. He tucked the paper in his pocket. "As I said, it matters not, for it shall never be. My heart is of little importance."

Raised voices could be heard from somewhere down the hall.

"Your aunt Catherine is here," his mother said in answer to his questioning look. "Anne is with her but has taken to her room, whether it is due to ill health or a need to avoid her mother, I am uncertain."

Just then, Lady Catherine stomped into the sitting room. "He is as unreasonable as ever!"

"I am not being unreasonable. You are being daft. To accept such connections into the family without some censure? And after he did not marry Anne as we had planned?" Lord Matlock threw his hands up as if unable to fathom the thoughts.

"It would be better for Anne to marry someone with higher connections," said Lady Catherine, "a peer or the son of a peer." Her eyes came to rest on Richard. "Even a second son would do."

A sly smile spread slowly across Lord Matlock's face. "That is an idea. It would keep all the landholdings within the family." He clapped his hands together and rubbed them back and forth. "I shall have my solicitor draw up the arrangement. Shall we have the wedding in two months? I do think that would give enough time to find him a replacement with his unit and ready the necessary items for the release of his inheritance, but I will have to defer to my solicitor and man of business for advice before we finalize the date." He leveled a hard glare at Richard. "Any objection shall be met with a significant, if not permanent breach. Do I make myself clear?"

Richard shook his head in disbelief. "I am no more to you than that?"

"On the contrary," said his father, "you are of great significance, and that is why your future must be secured. Were something to ever happen to your brother, you would need to secure the title with an appropriate heir, one with an acceptable lineage."

Richard's jaw clenched. "So I am a well-bred horse in your stable then, whose only expectation is to sire the next prize stallion. And if I do not, I, like that horse, shall be turned out to work along-side the other workhorses on the estate."

His father's eyes narrowed. "Not on my estates." His voice held more than a little warning.

Richard stepped closer and pulled himself up to his full height, which was two inches taller than his father. "And if you turn me out and something happens to my brother, then where will your precious title fall? Ah, yes, to your brother." The comment caused the reaction he desired. His father took a step back and his face paled slightly. "Two weeks," Richard said. "I ask two weeks to consider your offer, sir."

"What is there to consider?" said Lady Catherine.

"The value of my life," Richard snarled. He

moved toward the door, but his mother's hand on his arm forestalled him.

"I will see you again?" Her eyes were filled with fear.

"At least once more," he murmured as he kissed her cheek before leaving the room and instructing that his things be readied for a journey.

Acknowledgements

There are many who have had a part in the creation of this story. Some have read and commented on it. Some have proofread for grammatical errors and plot holes. Others have not even read the story and a few, I know, will never read it. However, their encouragement and belief in my ability, as well as their patience when I became cranky or when supper was late or the groceries ran low, was invaluable.

And so, I would like to say *thank you* to Zoe, Rose, Kristine, Ben, and Kyle. I feel blessed through your help, support, and understanding.

I have not listed my dear husband in the above group because, to me, he deserves his own special thank you, for, without his somewhat pushy insistence that I start sharing my writing, none of my writing goals and dreams would have been met.

Other Leenie B Books

You can find all of Leenie's books at this link
bit.ly/LeenieBBooks
where you can explore the collections below

~*~

Other Pens, Mansfield Park

~*~

Touches of Austen Collection

~*~

Other Pens, Pride and Prejudice

~*~

Dash of Darcy and Companions Collection

~*~

Marrying Elizabeth Series

~*~

Willow Hall Romances

~*~

The Choices Series

~*~

Darcy Family Holidays

~*~

Darcy and... An Austen-Inspired Collection

About the Author

Leenie Brown has always been a girl with an active imagination, which, while growing up, was both an asset, providing many hours of fun as she played out stories, and a liability, when her older sister and aunt would tell her frightening tales. At one time, they had her convinced Dracula lived in the trunk at the end of the bed she slept in when visiting her grandparents!

Although it has been years since she cowered in her bed in her grandparents' basement, she still has an imagination which occasionally runs away with her, and she feeds it now as she did then — by reading!

Her heroes, when growing up, were authors, and the worlds they painted with words were (and still are) her favourite playgrounds! Now, as an adult, she spends much of her time in the Regency world, playing with the characters from her favourite Jane Austen novels and those of her own creation.

When she is not traipsing down a trail in an attempt to keep up with her imagination, Leenie resides in the beautiful province of Nova Scotia with her two sons and her very own Mr. Brown (a wonderful mix of all the best of Darcy, Bingley, and Edmund with a healthy dose of the teasing Mr. Tilney and just a dash of the scolding Mr. Knightley).

Connect with Leenie

E-mail:
LeenieBrownAuthor@gmail.com
Facebook:
www.facebook.com/LeenieBrownAuthor
Blog:
leeniebrown.com
Patreon:
https://www.patreon.com/LeenieBrown
Subscribe to Leenie's Mailing List:
Book News from Leenie Brown
(bit.ly/LeenieBBookNews)

39756127R00144

Made in the USA
San Bernardino, CA
21 June 2019